It was an old family friend who got Carolus Deene embroiled in this latest case of his. Helena Gort, well on in her sixties, was staying at Cat's Cradle, a guesthouse by the sea; things had been going seriously wrong at Cat's Cradle . . . two deaths adjudged respectively as 'natural causes' and 'suicide' . . . resulting in "an atmosphere—not disagreeable so much as disturbing".

The story opens with Helena calling on Carolus and begging him to come with her to stay at Cat's Cradle, so that he can use his redoubtable gifts of detection and solve any crime or crimes there may have been and prevent any worse calamity. For there was no doubt in Helena's mind that something sinister had happened and something very unpleasant was brewing.

She was right.

D1564094

NOTHING
LIKE
BLOOD

by

LEO BRUCE

Academy
Chicago
Publishers

Published in 1985 by

Academy Chicago Publishers
425 N. Michigan Ave.
Chicago, IL 60611

Printed and bound in the USA

Library of Congress Cataloging in Publication Data

Bruce, Leo. 1903–1980.
    Nothing like blood.

    I. Title.
PR6005.R673N6   1985   823'.912   85-1363
ISBN 0-89733-128-1
ISBN 0-89733-127-3 (pbk.)

1

"The Coroner's Inquest called it suicide," said Mrs Gort.

"Then it probably was suicide," Carolus Deene told her. "Coroners are not the gullible men popularly supposed. They are usually shrewd and experienced."

"You may, of course, be right. In fact on the evidence it is hard to see how it could have been anything else. But I had been living in the house for some weeks when it happened, and I must say I find it all very odd. So much so that I have come to tell you about it."

"I appreciate that, my dear Helena."

"It won't be the first story I've told you. When you were a rather tiresome small boy you preferred stories to sweets, which was a bore."

Carolus smiled at his visitor, an old friend of his mother. She must be well on in her sixties, he thought, as mentally tough as old boots but kind and understanding, too. She had been one of those adventurous women who made arduous journeys in dangerous places and wrote lively books about them. She never had the fame of a Rosita Forbes or a Dorothy Mills but she was respected in her time for the accuracy of her reports. He had not seen her for years until now she was suddenly breaking the peace of his summer holidays by her visit.

"I can't say I much care either way," she went on now. "None of the people in this guest house—I suppose one must call it that—were friends of mine. But I think it will interest you. They are the sort of miscellaneous, rather peculiar, seemingly quite ordinary people who seem to attract you. I've read accounts of your various investiga-

5

:ions and, as soon as I had taken a look at Cat's Cradle—
that's the name of the place—and its inhabitants, I found
myself saying: 'This is just Carolus Deene's cup of tea.'
You see there was talk of a murder before this happened."

"What do you mean?"

"Well, a guest died there a month or two before. Quite
normally, of heart disease, I gathered. A married woman
who had been told by her doctors that she hadn't long
to live. Everything quite in order. The husband in hospital at the time and an experienced doctor perfectly
satisfied. Yet, when I reached the place, I found them all
on edge. Some of them quite jittery."

"But why?"

"It was hard to tell. There was an atmosphere of suspicion and intrigue. They all wanted to tell me, a newcomer, something or other about what had happened or
what they suspected. I was so interested that I decided to
keep a little journal of what went on."

"You did? And you're going to let me see it?"

"Of course. What do you think I've come here for? I
hope it will enable you to judge whether the Coroner's
verdict was right or not."

"You're splendid, Helena. I've never been handed a
potential case on such a gold platter. A journal, and kept
by someone with as keen an eye as yours. Did the people
in the house know you were keeping it?"

"Yes. There was an attempt to steal or destroy or perhaps just to read it. But it only seemed to make them
readier to talk to me."

Carolus nodded. "It would. What exhibitionists we all
are, criminals or not! Did you ever read that story about
the man who got himself a reputation of secretly keeping
a second Pepys's diary? He was flooded with invitations
and the most unexpected people brought out witticisms
which they practically told him to write down. When he

6

died it was discovered that his famous diary consisted of laundry bills and household accounts."

"They certainly gave me the full treatment," said Helena Gort. She used slang, out-of-date and up-to-the-minute, with no self-consciousness at all. "For what it's worth you can read it tonight."

"You speak of the atmosphere of this place. Was it really threatening?"

"I did not feel threatened. But some of them did, I think. Not the one on whom the inquest was. She didn't feel threatened at all—which you will understand, I suppose. But there certainly was a sense of danger in the air. I found it rather exhilarating. At my age one isn't startled by the squeak of a mouse. One has formed one's protective fatalism."

"I wonder what made you choose this place?"

"I had some work to do. Friends of mine were there last year and described it as quiet and comfortable. So it was, when they were there."

"Yet, in two months, there have been two deaths, both of women, which have both, as I understand it, caused some considerable discussion, at any rate. The first of heart disease, the second by a fall from a window."

"Not exactly from a window. From a little stone balcony before a window. And, anyway, her fall was watched, don't forget."

"From below. From a boat on the water."

"But they have made tests, Carolus. It seems that the creature was alone at the window. The people in the boat who saw it describe her as diving into space."

"Perhaps she did. It's not an uncommon form of suicide."

Helena Gort looked doubtful. "I have my reasons for doubting it," she said, "and you'll learn them when you come to read my journal."

"You mean you think she was murdered?"

"I don't see how. But I can't believe it was suicide."

"And the first death?"

"I've no opinion about that. It was before my time, as they say."

"You don't think they're connected?"

"It will take all your ingenuity, I think, to connect them."

They were interrupted by the entrance of Mrs Stick, Carolus's small hearted and severe housekeeper, who cooked superbly but was apt to extend her sharp authority over his life. She disapproved of his 'getting mixed up', as she called it, in 'murders and that', feeling that it damaged his reputation and her own, particularly in the view of her sister, who was married to a Battersea undertaker.

It seemed that Mrs Gort's years and previous acquaintance with Carolus's mother absolved her in Mrs Stick's mind from any suspicion of complicity in such things, and it was with something that tried to be a smile round the corners of her tight mouth that she asked whether Mrs Gort would be staying to dinner.

"Why don't you let Mrs Stick make you comfortable for the night, Helena? Then I could drive you back to your place tomorrow."

"Why not, indeed?" said Helena. "It's an excellent idea. Then you can take a look at . . ." Carolus tried to stop her but it was too late ". . . the suspects."

A change came over Mrs Stick. "The spare room's ready," she admitted sourly. "I'll see about the dinner."

"What have we?" asked Carolus, trying to cover Helena's gaffe by chattiness.

"There's a sooff-lay," admitted Mrs Stick. "Then some treat oh blue. Capon oh grow sell."

"You've certainly done us proud, Mrs Stick. *Soufflé, Truites au bleu* and *capon au gros sel*," he interpreted.

8

"I thought the lady was a friend of your mother's," snapped Mrs Stick, "and not come about anything of that sort. You needn't think I didn't hear because there it was —'suspects'. I was only saying to Stick, if we have any more of this, murders and I don't know what not, we shall have to give notice. There's my sister to think about as well as us, and goodness knows it's bad enough for me and Stick, never knowing when someone who's come to see you isn't going to pull a corpse out of his bag."

"But, as far as we know, there has *been* no murder," said Carolus reassuringly.

"There soon will have been if you get mixed up in it, that's a sure thing," said Mrs Stick. "And more than one, for all I know. I don't know why you can't be satisfied with the teaching."

When she had gone Helena Gort said: "My curiosity is roused by something else. Why 'the teaching' at all? Your father must have left you enough to live on without spending your time in a small obscure school trying to interest dull boys in history."

Carolus smiled. "My headmaster would be most distressed to hear you call the Queen's School, Newminster, small and obscure. The boys in it are no duller than any others. As for money, my father left me repulsively rich. All the more reason, as I see it, for doing a job, and teaching history is one of the very few things I can do."

"And, apparently, elucidate the more intricate of crimes."

"I never quite know why. It started when I wrote a book in which I reconsidered some historical misdoings —*Who Killed William Rufus?* It was rather idiotically called that by a publisher who thought up this title as most attractive. From that it was a short step to the contemporary and I have found myself involved again and again, sometimes by chance, sometimes through my own

9

curiosity, and sometimes because friends or acquaintances have brought me things. As you have."

"You were always an inquisitive little boy. You used to say you wanted to be an explorer. I suppose that's what you are, in a way, only in darker places than I ever visited, the deep gulleys and ravines of a murderer's mind."

"Really, Helena, you're becoming quite literary. In fact, what I find so disturbing about the whole thing is that murderers' minds are so very much like those of other people. If they had a special mentality, something easily distinguished from our own so that as soon as one saw their reactions one could recognize them like the footprints of the abominable snowman, it would be so much more comforting. But, except for the fact that they kill someone, they seem to behave in a perfectly commonplace way. It makes any kind of investigation both more difficult and more destructive of one's faith in people."

"I see that. In this case, for instance, if there has been a murder, or even two murders, the guilty person or persons can scarcely be from outside. And a more unmurderous lot than the guests and staff it would be hard to find. The owner, a Mrs Derosse, is a great hulking good-natured woman, and her niece who has just come to stay with her is charming. The staff consists of the Jerrisons, a married couple, with some outside help. I don't know much about Jerrison, who seems quiet and efficient, but the wife's a garrulous person, far too garrulous to have any secrets, one would think. There is a retired colonial bishop and his sister, two retired schoolmistresses and so on—mostly well-to-do people who don't want to bother to keep up homes of their own. One of the things that makes one inclined to accept the Coroner's verdict is the extreme improbability of any of them doing anything criminal."

Carolus nodded. "It's nearly always like that," he said.

"I've no doubt you'll have no difficulty in finding a suspect . . ."

It was unfortunate, perhaps, that through the door behind Helena Mrs Stick had appeared at this moment with a tray of drinks. Her face was set in lines of fierce disapproval, but the tray went down without the least clatter and she said nothing as she withdrew.

"You think the police are satisfied?" asked Carolus when the door was shut.

"I have no means of knowing. They made very thorough interrogations before the inquest. They kept me for nearly half an hour. Very politely, I must say, but they did not mean to miss a thing. We have not seen anything of them since, but that is not to say they regard the case as closed, is it?"

"No. They have patience. Suppose that, when I've read your journal, I am interested. What are the chances of my being able to stay in the house?"

"There must be a room, because Christine Derosse has moved into Sonia's room—the one they call the room in the tower. The room she had before that must be unoccupied. But whether Mrs Derosse would let you have it or not, I don't know. She might be glad to do so."

"I have nothing to do for the rest of the holidays," said Carolus. "I want to give the Sticks a rest."

"Then shut your house and come. I think it will interest you, anyway. And if you find nothing, *that* would be a change, wouldn't it, after all your gory adventures?"

"It would be most refreshing. You say the people who watched this woman from the boat said she seemed to *dive* from the balcony. That's a curious word to use. Was there water directly below it?"

"At high tide, yes. But the tide was low. She fell on the rocks. Killed instantly."

" Could she possibly have thought the sea was up? "

" No. I am told that is impossible. She knew the place well and even at high tide the water barely covered the rocks and certainly was not deep enough for a dive from that height. And she was fully dressed. Yet the people watching are positive that she was alone on the balcony. They had been observing her sitting on the parapet brightly framed in the window. The lights in the room behind her shone out."

" Curious," said Carolus. " What about these people who saw it? "

" Holiday-makers. A couple from the holiday camp along the coast. Moonlight-boating."

" Oh. There was moonlight? "

" Yes. I understand so. I don't remember it myself. But the police took the couple out in a boat to what they estimated was the same spot and the lights in the room were turned on. No one knows what they think but their evidence at the inquest seemed to me to suggest that they were satisfied that the woman on the balcony must have been alone."

" Did anyone suggest that she might have simply over-balanced? That it was, in fact, an accident? "

" That was, of course, a supposition. But the evidence of the couple in the boat was against it."

" It seems far more probable than suicide."

" I suggest you ask me no more about it till you have read my diary of what came before. Then if there's any-thing more I can tell you, I will."

" All right, Helena. I daresay you're tired of the whole thing."

" Not a bit. I'm most interested. A great deal has hap-pened to me in a reasonably varied life, but nothing like this. Give me another drink."

It was not until he was in bed that Carolus opened the

bulky notebook which Helena Gort had used for her diary. Had she bought it specially? he wondered. How soon had she realized that there was any reason to keep a diary? Wonderful woman—he was sure she would have noted the very things he wanted to know.

He arranged a pile of pillows, set the light so that it fell on Helena's fine angular handwriting, and began.

2

I ARRIVED here at four o'clock this afternoon and I am already mystified. What was intended to be a quiet month in a seaside guest house among commonplace middle-aged people looks like turning into something very different and perhaps not altogether pleasant. I will try to explain what makes me think this.

First, lest you should suppose these are the imaginings of a nervous old lady, let me explain about myself. I am, perhaps, old, being sixty-two, and I haven't the least objection to being called a lady, but I am not at all nervous. My name is scarcely remembered now, for the eight books I have written have not had any popular success though my *Travels in French Equatorial Africa* had a certain *succès d'estime* before the war. I am in the best of health and always full of energy. I am considered a down-to-earth sort of person and have, I hope, a sense of humour. I have no near relatives or responsibilities and my income is sufficient but not lavish.

I came to this place because some acquaintances of mine were here last year and found it comfortable. The house is called Cat's Cradle and it is a long, flat, plain-looking house built on a rocky headland so that the rooms on the south side look across the bay, while those on the narrow eastern end of the house look straight out to sea, with a cliff below them. It is not a huge or forbidding cliff, but one can look down from the stone balconies, perhaps fifty feet, to the rocks below or, at high tide, to the water which scarcely covers them. The house is supposed to have been built by an eccentric millionaire, but I have noticed that in England anyone who creates a home which is not exactly like everyone else's is an eccentric millionaire. There is nothing eccentric about Cat's Cradle; it is solidly built of stone on rock foundations and although the architecture might be described as Victorian rococo, the site is magnificent.

I came here to work. To my surprise, a travel book of mine which I thought almost forgotten is to be re-issued in a paperback edition and I want to revise it thoroughly before it goes to press. I wrote to Mrs Derosse, the proprietress, and received a very pleasant and sensible letter giving me her terms, which are not excessive. It seems she prefers permanent lettings and runs the place chiefly for people who for one reason or another do not want to keep up homes of their own. She had a vacancy for the last half of August and the whole of September and I took it.

She warned me that the nearest town is Belstock, three miles away, and that there is nothing between Cat's Cradle and that except a holiday camp. "But that doesn't trouble us," she added, "as the inmates have their own amusements within the camp and rarely leave it." It all sounded ideal and I looked forward to days of quiet work in my room, with perhaps some good Bridge in the evening.

My first surprise was Mrs Derosse herself. I had pictured her a neat, businesslike, busy woman. She is enormous, loud, good-natured and—this will sound absurd till I explain more fully—frightened. I knew it before I had been with her five minutes. She is by nature a self-assured type, yet, while we were talking, she had that curious absent air which you find in people who are afraid of what may happen next. She seemed to be listening for something, though not anything specific.

Moreover, she has a past. It is not a very shameful one and she told it me quite readily when I gave her an opportunity. She was in the circus. I happened to mention that her name reminded me of a famous circus star I remembered seeing in Milan many years ago, who was billed as Leon de Rossi.

"That was my husband," she said. "And if you saw him you must have seen me because I was in the act."

I did seem to remember a dark buxom girl and I pretended to recognize her at once. She was delighted and for a moment lost that air of apprehension. It was then she said that her guests knew she had been in the circus and she sometimes wondered what they thought.

"It's not that it's anything to be ashamed of," she said. "Quite the contrary. My niece is still in the business and was at Olympia last year. It's just that the clientèle here are well . . . rather stuffy sort of people, if you know what I mean. Mostly retired, quiet, elderly. They may not like it. And anyhow, just lately . . ."

She stopped and I said: "Yes?"

"Nothing, really. There's been rather a change since your friends were here last year."

"In what way?"

"It's hard to explain. I think it's since Mrs Mallister died. However, you don't want to hear about that."

Of course my curiosity was aroused and I *did* want to hear about that, but I thought it better not to ask direct questions.

"I didn't know you'd had a death in the house," I said.

"Yes, yes. Two months ago," she answered rather impatiently. "Mrs Mallister." She said no more.

I went with her to see my room, which is delightful. I have a sea view, but not the sheer one from the rooms on the east end.

At tea, which was in the room called the lounge, I met several of my fellow guests. There were a Major Natterley and his wife, a retired colonial bishop with his sister, and two women, Miss Godwin and Miss Grey, who it seems are not related but have lived together for thirty years and are, inevitably I suppose, called by Mrs Derosse The Gee-Gees. There was also Mr Mallister, the widower of the lady whose death seems to have marked the 'change' in life at Cat's Cradle. More guests were promised at dinner time, but I felt these were quite enough to go on with.

We chatted with the most idiotic clichés. Had I had a nice journey? Wasn't the weather wonderful so late in August? Miss Godwin or Miss Grey—I haven't yet learned to distinguish them—had read one of my books and said I must have had a most *interesting* life, and so on. Here, too, I was conscious of something behind the conversation, as it were, as though everyone thought there were eavesdroppers.

Yet there was nothing extraordinary about the people in themselves. The only mystery about Bishop Grissell is why he should have retired, for he seems to be in the prime of life. A tall, sinewy man with a deep voice, he has fierce little tufts of hair and powerful, tanned features. He is bald, but over his ears and eyes, from his lobes and nostrils, on his wrists and neck, black hair sprouts and he looks muscular and stringy. His sister whom he calls 'Phiz, my dear'—or is it 'Fizz, my dear'?—is tall, too. She has shared his travels and looks as though she has been carried in a sedan chair in tropical climates: a downright, rather aggressive woman who gave me piercing stares and, when my book was mentioned, said: "I never read books by women."

I said: "Oh, why not?" as though I was deeply interested and she replied simply: "Waste of time."

The Natterleys speak only in terms of 'we', a habit which, carried to extremes by married couples, seems to me rather tiresome. They are much concerned with explaining their dislikes and disapprovals. 'We don't care for that sort of thing.' 'We shouldn't wish to do that.' They must find life difficult. "We never eat cucumber in any form," one of them said when they were handed the sandwiches. "We don't believe in eating between meals," explained the other. He is small and dressy while she has been very pretty, I think, and would be still, if the corners of her mouth did not go down in perpetual disapproval.

As for the Gee-Gees, one is timid and rather sweet, the other of sterner stuff but not in the least pushing. They were schoolmistresses until one of them—I shall know which in time—inherited rather a lot of money and they gave up teaching to travel. They moved about for many years, seeing all the places they had talked about in geography lessons, and have been at Cat's Cradle longer than anyone else.

The widower has remained here. He is a small, modest, smiling man in his forties with a kind face and quiet voice, a favourite with Mrs Derosse, I gather. He has good manners and was apt to be somewhat attentive to me. Not quite ingratiating—what is called 'nice'.

If the undertone of disturbance or apprehension, or whatever it is, does not only exist in my imagination, if it is anything more than a hunch of mine, I mean, then my first impression is that it is not directly connected with any of these. They are rather the kind of people one would expect to find in a fairly expensive guest house in a healthy situation, and, when I left them after tea, I found myself looking forward with some interest to meeting what Bishop Grissell calls ' the younger faction '. This I did before dinner.

None of the men actually get into dinner-jackets for this, but there is a good deal of rather self-conscious ' changing ', and first and second gongs are sounded. How Mrs Derosse gets staff I can't think—bribery, I suppose— but the ' backbone ' of it, she told me, is a married couple who have been with her some years and ' really,' she says, ' they might just as well be my partners. They do better out of it than I do.' But Jerrison, the man who waits at table, seems efficient, and his wife—I judge from this evening's meal—is a good cook.

At seven there is a gathering in the lounge and Jerrison serves drinks, mainly sherry, I noticed; he has a little serving-bar in the entrance hall which he opens at this time. I don't know what kind of licence Mrs Derosse has, but imagine these drinks are considered ' with meals '. I asked for a pink gin and Jerrison gave me a snorter.

While I was drinking this, Sonia Reid came in. She is very nearly beautiful—thirty-two or -three, I should say, a good figure and a vivid sensual face. She is, I decided at once, the *femme fatale* of this little party. She chatted with me amicably, keeping her fine dark eyes on mine as she did so. I felt she was sizing me up, not as a person but as I might affect her. Could I be of any possible interest? Did my arrival constitute a threat to anything she wanted? All this while she talked about the garden, and how impossible it was to make anything grow in these salt sea winds.

But Sonia Reid is not the only woman at Cat's Cradle who might claim to be attractive, as I realized when Esmée Welton appeared—a very different style, but good-

18

looking all the same. She is small, full of character, intelligent and dresses with flair.

Both Sonia Reid and Esmée Welton work. Esmée is the manageress of a big dress shop in Belstock—quite an important affair. Sonia is in partnership with a man, owning what was once a small music shop but is now a much larger business dealing in television and radio as well as gramophone records and musical instruments. She is supposed to be a fine pianist.

Then there is Steve Lawson. Why he should choose to live in this place I cannot imagine. He is believed to be rich, idle and under forty. He drives a Jaguar and there was some vague reference this evening to one of his horses which had run, or not run, somewhere. He is just what one would expect, fleshy but handsome, with one of those rich plummy voices which sound as though they are lubricated with fine old brandy.

There was only one thing in the general conversation this evening which seemed at all significant. A pianist, I think, or a violinist—I could not gather details because I was being boomed at by the bishop—is coming to give a concert at Belstock and is going to play somebody's 'Third'; an artist, I imagine, of great eminence and popularity.

Mallister, the widower, said in a perfectly even voice with no suggestion of morbidity: "How Lydia would have enjoyed that!" An ordinary remark, one would have said, of no more interest than the rest of the conversation.

It produced an instant effect. The bishop forgot his missionary efforts and there was, for at least five seconds, complete silence. That may not sound much but the effect was dramatic. Even Jerrison, who was handing some vegetables to Mrs Natterley, looked across at Mallister. Then, as pointedly as it had stopped, conversation was hastily resumed and everyone seemed to think of something to say. The bishop continued to describe his journey up country—in a canoe, I remember—and Sonia Reid suddenly wanted to know from Steve Lawson whether she should back Lighthouse-keeper on Saturday.

I ought to have explained how the dining-room is arranged. There is one large table, at which Mrs Derosse presides, and two small ones. At the large table the bishop sits on Mrs Derosse's right, I am next to him, then Mallister, Sonia Reid, Steve Lawson, Esmée Welton and 'Phiz' Grissell. The Natterleys have a table to themselves, so do the Gee-Gees. When Mallister dropped what appears to have been an unconscious bombshell, the Gee-Gees and the Natterleys looked across with as much alarm as the rest. It was quite extraordinary.

I decided to be as innocent as he and deliberately put my foot in it. "Was your wife musical, Mr Mallister?" I asked, during a pause for mastication during the bishop's talk of adventures.

No one else seemed to notice this.

"She was, very," said Mallister. "Until she became an invalid during the last year of her life she was a fine violinist." Then he added, in his matter-of-fact way: "She died quite recently, you know."

"Yes, I had heard that. Was it her heart?"

"Yes, heart. Heart," he said hurriedly. "She had been under sentence of death for some time. But she had great courage, as the doctors admitted, and insisted on knowing the truth. Dr Cuffley told me she could not live for more than a few weeks, and he had called in two specialists for consultation. Then, unfortunately, I had to go into hospital myself for an operation and I was away from her when the end came. However, it must be thought of as a release. She had suffered a great deal."

As he talked, the room became silent, not suddenly as before, but as though other conversations slowly lost interest in competition with this one. Mallister's fellow-guests seemed to wish not to listen but could not help themselves.

" Tragic," I said politely.

" She was not old, you see," went on Mallister. I have gathered since that this open confidence was most uncharacteristic of the man, who is apt to be self-effacing. " We had neither of us reached the cross-roads of fifty; but it seems that, once the heart ceases to function normally, medical science is powerless."

" That's true," said Bishop Grissell. " I remember one of my ablest men in Mashonaland . . ." Or was it Matabele? Or Madagascar or Mauritius, Mozambique or Mombasa? It began with M and didn't end at all, at least not for the rest of the meal.

Over coffee in the lounge I waited hopefully for a mention of Bridge. Neither Steve Lawson nor Sonia Reid appeared and after some minutes we heard his Jaguar start up in the drive. The Gee-Gees do beautiful *petit point* and got down to it before the coffee-things were removed. I was sitting near the Natterleys and asked them if they played.

" No, we never play card games," one of them said, as though I had made an improper suggestion. I might have known what answer I should get. I gather that they have their own sitting-room and only stay in the lounge after dinner for a few moments—' We don't wish to appear stand-offish.'

" We used to play at one time," Mallister told me. " Lydia liked a game. But lately, somehow, there has never been a four. We must see what we can do. Mrs Derosse plays excellently."

Conversation grew desultory after that. The bishop attacked the crossword in an evening paper, while Phiz read a book—by a man, I presumed.

It was a warm evening and I decided to take a stroll. I went up to my room for a coat and on the way met a large woman, the first happy-looking person I had seen at Cat's Cradle.

"I'm Mrs Jerrison, the housekeeper," she told me. "Let me know if there's anything you want, won't you?"

She had a round, red face and looked countrified and comfortable. I liked her at once. I felt, too, rather mischievously, that here would probably be the source of gossip from whom I should learn all.

"Thank you," I said. "I'm sure everything is quite all right."

I meant my room, of course, but as I made this silly remark I wondered whether she would see any *double entendre*. She did not appear to, though she hesitated for a moment before wishing me good night.

As there was only one other small incident this evening which could be described as significant, it may seem that I am 'seeing things' after all. I can only say that there is no question in my mind. Something very unpleasant has happened or is about to happen in this house, and all these people were aware of it. It hangs about the place like a mist. Perhaps I was wrong in using the word 'fear'. Mrs Derosse is afraid of something, but it may only be a threat to her business. The rest of them are . . . on edge, apprehensive perhaps, or perhaps only curious. Whatever it is, it seems to be connected with the late Lydia Mallister. I shall try to ask no questions and in time, I feel, I shall know a great deal more. I do not deny for a moment that my curiosity is roused.

The incident I mentioned was scarcely an incident at all, yet it surprised me. On my way back from my walk I saw two people coming rather fast from the house. They were in the light of an overhead electric bulb and were visible to me before they saw me, I think, for they were talking with some animation and suddenly became silent as they approached. There was nothing furtive about them, for they had come from the front door which they slammed behind them.

They paused to speak to me—James Mallister and Esmée Welton. Been for a stroll? That sort of thing.

"We take a constitutional to the top of the cliff," said Mallister casually.

"Every evening?" I asked.

"Most evenings," said Esmée, "unless it's pouring."

"I'd like to come with you another evening," I told them.

They accepted this with just a little more enthusiasm than was natural in the circumstances, particularly if there *are* any circumstances.

So I came up to bed. It occurred to me to look up 'Cat's Cradle' in Brewer's *Dictionary of Phrase and Fable*. I shall surely be thought imaginative when I say that the definition suggested to me, in an obscure way, something rather sinister. 'A game played with a piece of twine by two children,' it reads.

3

On this my second day at Cat's Cradle I have learned a great deal more about my fellow guests and am delighted to find that the impression I had of an unusual atmosphere in the place is not my own fancy.

I decided to go into Belstock by bus this afternoon and just as the bus was about to leave its starting point near the house I saw Mrs Jerrison hurrying towards it. I turned round and greeted her and asked her to sit with me, which she did. She was out of breath at first, for she is a biggish woman and had hurried over the last hundred yards, but she soon recovered herself and to my secret pleasure she began without hesitation to talk about the household.

All I needed to do was to put in every now and again a 'Really?' or 'How extraordinary!' and since a good deal of what she told me *was* extraordinary, this was easy.

I started her off by saying it seemed that Mrs Mallister's death had made a difference to Cat's Cradle since my friends were there last year.

"It's not so much her *death* made a difference," said Mrs Jerrison. "It was how it happened and the money."

I had been wondering when we should come to a mention of money and spoke my first "Really?" in an interested, almost incredulous, gasping sort of way.

"Yes. You see we all knew it was her had the money. She never made any secret of it, and you can always tell. But we never knew it was that amount."

I longed to ask 'What amount?' but resisted it.

"When it came out it was quite a shock. Nothing for him, though he had all the life insurance which, by what I can hear, is a good many thousand pounds. She couldn't leave that away from him because it was in his name all along, but all the rest she did. Even that Miss Grissell, being an old friend of hers—well, school-friends they were—got I don't know how many thousands, and she didn't forget Jerrison and me. Not by a nice sum, she didn't. That's what's caused a lot of the talk.

"He's never said a word out of place, though. Mr Mallister, I mean. 'It was Lydia's money,' he told Mrs Derosse, 'and it was for her to decide what she wanted to do with it. She knew I was amply provided for by the insurance on her life, for which we had been paying an enormous premium.' No, he's never said a word against her, from what I've been told. But I thought her will was spiteful. Really I did. She only made it a month or two before she died."

I was assimilating all this so eagerly that I had not noticed we were coming into the outskirts of Belstock.

"You know what it was, don't you?" A rhetorical question, I thought, if ever there was one. "It was him going about with that Esmée Welton. That's what put her back up. I don't know whether they thought she didn't know, or what, but they were running off together morning, noon and night . . ."

"Night?" I questioned bravely.

"Well, quite late enough, it was. He works in a bank in Belstock and she's manageress of a shop I'll show you presently, so it's ten to one they used to meet here every day. And she must have got to hear. I shouldn't be surprised if it wasn't that Sonia told her, because she and Mrs Mallister got very thick towards the end. Oh, very thick, they got. Sonia was up in her room at all hours. Well, here we are at the bus stop and I don't suppose you want to hear all this. Only you did ask whether things hadn't changed since your friends were here and I had to tell you."

"Of course I want to hear, Mrs Jerrison. It's all most interesting. I wonder whether perhaps you'd have tea with me, if there's somewhere nice? Then you can tell me all about it."

"To tell you the truth, it's a relief to, because my husband won't talk about it, and there are times when I have to say something or bust with what's going on, and there's no one up there I feel like talking to about it. Yes, there's a nice café on the front. The Sunnyside, it's called. Not two minutes from here. What I was going to say is that Sonia very likely put a spoke in, hoping for something herself, I daresay, though, if so, she was disappointed. It turned out this last will was made before she got so thick with Mrs Mallister, else there might have been."

"But, Mrs Jerrison," I managed to interpolate, "Mrs Mallister died quite naturally . . ."

"If you *call* that natural," conceded Mrs Jerrison. "It was her heart, they said, and the doctor gave a certificate straight away. Well, so it may have been her heart, but that's not to say someone didn't do something to help things on a little, is it? This is the Sunnyside. Nice, isn't it? It's kept by three ladies and they make ever such nice cakes and that. I mean there are heart attacks and heart attacks, aren't there? And no one knew about this new will, from what I've been told."

"Are you really suggesting that Mrs Mallister was murdered?"

"I wouldn't go as far as to say that. Not in so many words. But I'd like to know what *is* going on in that house if something didn't happen. I mean you can see for yourself the way they carry on. All looking at one another as though they didn't know what to think. And the whispering and that. Poor Mrs Derosse is nearly out of her mind, that I do know. I was glad when I saw you yesterday because I could tell at once you weren't the sort to get in a fluster about it. I make Jerrison lock our doors at night, that's one thing. We're nearly always the last up—neither of us liking to go to bed early. Still even then I lock the door. I wouldn't stay if it wasn't for his lungs. The doctors have told him, you know, and this place just suits him. But it's not nice and I can't help wondering what's going to happen next."

"If you seriously think someone caused Mrs Mallister's death, you must have some idea who it was?"

"Well, it wasn't Mr Mallister, that's a sure thing, because he was in hospital at the time having an operation.

26

Jerrison had only been to see him that afternoon and took him some books. More than two weeks he'd been there when it happened and he couldn't come to the funeral or anything. It was another ten days before he was back. He didn't seem to say much at the time, but lately he's taken to talking about her whenever he gets a chance. I think he was fond of her in his way, only he's quiet, you know."

"Then who . . . ?"

"Well, it might have been almost any of them, mightn't it?"

"I can't see why you should think so. Mrs Mallister was dangerously ill and her doctor found nothing questionable in her death."

"It's not that. It's the way they carry on now. If there was nothing wrong, why do they all look as though they've seen a ghost? You hear little bits, too. There was a big row between those Natterleys and Sonia Reid the other night. I heard it myself. I was just passing the lounge at the time when I heard them. 'All I can say is,' I heard the Major pipe up, 'all I can say is, if it's a co-incidence, it's a very extraordinary one. And why did you have to go all the way to London for that?' 'Don't be ridiculous,' said Sonia. 'I happened to be in London and got them there. And I don't see what on earth it's got to do with you.' 'This affair is to do with all of us,' said Mrs Natterley; 'you don't think we like being mixed up in it, do you?' That's all I heard, but it's enough, isn't it? And it's like that all the time. My husband's worried, I can see that, though I can't get him to say much. He did tell me once that it got on his nerves the way they stopped talking whenever he came into a room."

I poured the tea and it brought a pause in Mrs Jerrison's fascinating narrative. But not a long pause.

"There's another thing I don't like," she said, "though

I never so much as gave it a thought before all this happened. There's two of the bedrooms look out over the cliff. A sheer drop it is. I don't know whether you've seen it?"

"Yes . . ."

"And both have got little balconies to them. If anyone was to fall from there it would be certain death, high tide or low."

"You mean suicide?"

"I don't know what I mean, but I don't like it. Who'd be to say what it was if one of them went? Any more than with Mrs Mallister."

"Who occupy those rooms?"

"One's right at the top. They call it the room in the tower because it's built above the other. It's not really a tower, though it has a staircase of its own. That's Sonia Reid's. Under her is Mrs Derosse's own room. Of course there's something between Sonia and Steve Lawson. Well, there has been for a long while. We used to think they were going to get married at one time but, since this has happened, I don't know. They seem to be arguing half the time. He's supposed to be rich, but I often wonder. He doesn't seem to do anything for a living and, as I said to my husband, you can't go *on* like that. He talks about his racehorses and that, but you never see his name in the papers. He's very often overdue in paying Mrs Derosse, I do know that. Of course it may not mean anything, but then again, it might."

"He seemed a very ordinary young man to me."

"Oh, they're all ordinary enough, or so I thought till this happened. That's what makes it so funny. I mean, if they don't like it, why don't they leave, instead of staying to watch one another?"

"Why should they, Mrs Jerrison? There has been nothing unpleasant like a police inquiry, has there?"

" No. I sometimes think it's a pity there hasn't; then we should know where we were, perhaps. The doctor saw Mrs Mallister . . ."

" The same night? "

" No. We didn't know anything about it till the morning. Mrs Smithers, the gardener's wife and one of my helps, took her in a cup of tea about nine o'clock and there she was. You could see she was dead before you got near her. The doctor was round in half an hour and the whole thing kept as quiet as possible. Well, it doesn't do in a guest house, does it? There wasn't even an inquest or anything. She was buried two days later and most of them went to the funeral though I wouldn't say she was liked. She had a wicked tongue, you know. I always got on with her all right and I will say I've only got cause to be grateful, but she did say things about people."

" I suppose she had a bell in her room? Or some way of calling if she needed attention in the night? "

" Certainly she had. Mrs Derosse had it fixed up as soon as Mr Mallister was going into hospital. It rang in Mrs Derosse's room and she couldn't help but hear it if it had been rung that night, but it wasn't. Whatever happened must have been too sudden for that. Anyway, Dr Cuffley who had been attending her for a long time was quite satisfied. And he's a good doctor, I will say that. I know when my husband was ill last winter . . ."

I was determined to keep her to the point.

" Yes. I've heard Dr Cuffley is good," I said. " And he never had any doubts? "

" No one had any doubts at the time. It all came afterwards."

" What started it? " I asked, wondering precisely what ' it ' might be.

" It's hard to say. Partly when we heard about the will, I suppose. People started remembering things. Mrs Derosse told me herself she thought she heard something in the night and, when she got up to see what it was, she saw that Sonia nipping up to her room. About half past twelve that was, she thought. But I think what really caused more talk than anything was when Mr Mallister came out of hospital."

"Really?"

"They didn't trouble to conceal it, I mean."

"Who?"

"Why, him and Esmée Welton. We'd always thought there was something but now they didn't seem to care who knew. Quite brazen about it, they are. I mean, you'd think they'd have the decency, with her scarcely cold. But no. I've seen them myself. The bishop and Miss Grissell don't like it. You can tell that. We know Miss Grissell's a bit blunt and that, and comes out with what she thinks, but I've never heard her carry on as she did to Mrs Derosse about it. 'Disgusting!' she said. 'Nothing short of disgusting!' Mrs Derosse kept very cool. 'I don't consider it any business of mine,' she said. That ought to have been enough but it wasn't. Not for Miss Grissell. 'It is of mine,' she said, very high and mighty. 'I was Lydia's oldest friend.' And she marched out of the room. I wish she'd have said it to me. I'd have told her to mind her own business. I will own Mr Mallister and Esmée never trouble to hide anything, but I suppose they think they've a right to do as they please. After all, she did cut him out of her will. But they say the bishop and his sister look like furies at Mr Mallister. And at Esmée. I believe they think she had something to do with Mrs Mallister's death."

"And you don't?"

"Think that? Well, I don't know what to think. Something went on that night we don't know about, and I do believe Mr Mallister and Esmée are quite silly about one another. I can't see who else can have wanted Mrs Mallister out of the way. But whether they'd do anything like that or not, I can't say. According to what I can hear, though, the bishop and his sister think so. In fact, Mrs Smithers, when she happened to be doing his room, did say she couldn't help seeing a letter addressed to the Chief Constable. What else could that have been, I should like to know?"

"It could have been an invitation to dinner, couldn't it?"

"Not from him. He's never invited anyone to anything in his life, if you ask me. Mean? You couldn't believe how mean he is. And his sister."

There was a significant silence while Mrs Jerrison left time for this to sink in. I was enjoying myself and had no intention of hurrying away but I could not help wondering why Mrs Jerrison had come into Belstock, if she was prepared to spend the whole afternoon in the Sunnyside Café, appeasing my curiosity. This seemed to occur to her, too.

"Well, I was going to do some shopping," she observed without moving, "but it must be late for that now. I've got to get back and do the dinner presently. Only, as I was saying, that Esmée isn't the only one suspected. I do know that. Miss Godwin and Miss Grey have got their ideas, too. They wouldn't say anything, mind you. They just believe in being civil with everyone, but keeping themselves to themselves—always have done ever since they came here. But Miss Godwin, that's the taller of the two, came out with it to me when I was up in her room one day. She's a bit more downright than the other. It's Miss Grey who's got the money, but you'd never know that. I happened to make a passing remark about Mrs Mallister's death, not meaning anything really, when Miss Godwin turned round and said: 'I don't know anything about it and I don't want to know.' 'Quite right, Miss

Godwin,' I said, 'nor do I, nor does my husband. It's just that you hear so much talk. Miss Grissell was only saying . . .' ' Miss Grissell! ' says Miss Godwin, quite fuming she was. 'I'd like to know what Miss Grissell was arguing about in Mrs Mallister's room that night! ' she said. It quite bowled me over. I could see the moment she'd said it she was sorry she'd let it slip out.''

" How did she know? '' I asked.

" Search me. Their room's next door but the walls are ever so thick. She wouldn't say any more then and never has since. But I've seen the way she looks at the bishop and his sister as though she was sorry for them.''

" And do you think anyone in turn has suspicions of her or Miss Grey? ''

" Of those two? No! Who could have? There couldn't be any reason for them to be mixed up in it, could there? They go their own way and never mix much with the others. It isn't as though they were friends of Mrs Mallister's. They knew her when she first came here and after she was laid up they'd call on her once in a way, but that was all. It was just that one remark Miss Godwin passed to me.''

As we left the café I asked one more question. " What do you think, then, Mrs Jerrison—about the future, I mean? I ask because I came here to do some work and I've found myself so interested in all you've told me that I wonder how I'm going to get down to work at all. Do you think it will just die down and be forgotten in time? ''

" No, I don't,'' said Mrs Jerrison promptly. " I think it's all leading to something and will end in a bust-up. Don't ask me how. Only I don't believe you can have a lot of people living in a house like that, all watching the others and thinking and suspecting, without something happening. What it'll be I don't know, but it gives me the creeps when I think about it. I'm glad you've come, though, and I've got someone to talk to. If I notice any-thing else, I'll let you know."

"Thank you; I'll do the same," I promised.

4

At dinner this evening there was a scene. We assembled as yesterday in the lounge. The drinks consumed at this hour are discreetly charged for by Jerrison, but that does not make the nightly occasion any less like that of a small provincial cocktail-party. For some time everything seemed normal. The bishop and Phiz had been playing golf and talked about it.

"Do you play golf?" I asked the Natterleys.

"Not here," said the Major. "We don't care much for the local club."

When we went into dinner only Sonia Reid was missing and Steve Lawson and I seemed alone in noticing this.

"Where's Sonia?" he asked of the gathering.

"I saw her come in," said Miss Godwin. "She was a little later than usual. I expect she'll be down in a minute."

But she did not appear while we swallowed—the bishop rather vigorously—an excellent *consommé*. I suppose Mrs Jerrison must have made it earlier, for it showed no sign of hasty work; it was clear and brown, like a good sherry.

When Sonia at last came in I could see she was in a state of high emotion, though I could not decide at first whether it was anger or distress. She took her place, motioned impatiently to Jerrison that she wanted no *consommé* and turned to our hostess. "Mrs Derosse," she said in a ringing voice, "someone has been in my room."

Mrs Derosse has a gift for looking quite blank when she likes. "Of course," she said, "Mrs Smithers . . ."

"I don't mean that. Mrs Smithers does it every morning and leaves it in perfect order. I don't mean Mrs Smithers. Someone else has been there, since then."

She kept her eyes on Mrs Derosse, but I had a feeling that her words were intended for someone else at the table, someone whose identity she knew or at least suspected. If she had taken one glance at anyone present she would have revealed this, but I could see she was taking care not to do so.

"Really, Sonia, are you sure?" said Mrs. Derosse rather feebly.

"Quite sure. You see I thought this might happen and took one or two precautions. There are things Mrs Smithers never touches—indeed I have given her instructions about them. They have been disturbed."

"Is anything missing?" asked Mrs Derosse.

Sonia gave a very unpleasant laugh. "No," she said. "The person who searched my room must have thought I was a nit-wit if he or she imagined for one moment that I would leave anything there."

Mrs Derosse became rather indignant. "No one has ever lost any property from a room here," she said, "in the eight years we have been open."

"I don't mean that," said Sonia. "I leave my bits and pieces about every day. This was a particular thing of value only to one person."

She was talking for the benefit of that one person, I knew. I looked round the table and found most of the guests busily eating, though Miss Godwin looked boldly across at Sonia. It was Steve Lawson who broke the short but uncomfortable silence. "What do you mean, Sonia? A document of some kind?"

She rounded on him as though relieved at not having to continue staring at Mrs Derosse.

"Never mind what I mean," she said angrily. Then she continued, but not quite so fixedly, towards Mrs Derosse.

"It's not very pleasant to find one's things disturbed," she said. "Someone must have been in my room for quite a considerable time. Even a suitcase has been opened."

"I'm very sorry, Sonia," said Mrs Derosse, "but I'm quite sure it was not one of the staff."

"I'm not saying it was," said Sonia; "in fact I'm certain it wasn't. But that only makes it worse, in a way. Does it mean we've got to have locks on our doors?"

The bishop obliged. "I remember once in Zanzibar . . ." Or was it Zululand, the Zambesi, Zomba or Zesfontein? "I remember a man finding that his luggage, which he had left most carefully fastened and sealed . . ." his story drew us into the comparative calm of Africa. I heard no more at that time of the search of Sonia's room.

After dinner there was a surprise for me. I was approached by Mrs Natterley. "We wondered whether you would care to take coffee in our little sitting-room?" she said.

I accepted at once.

"We prefer it to the lounge. It is not cold enough for a fire yet but even in this weather we like having somewhere of our own we can retreat to." She actually smiled and I thought again how pretty she could be.

Their sitting-room is small but they have some quite lovely things, not collected, I thought, during the Major's years of foreign service, but English, most of them of the eighteenth century. They saw me looking about, as I can never refrain from doing in an interesting room.

"When we gave up our home," said Dora Natterley, "there were some things we couldn't be parted from. We

35

simply cannot bear modern furniture. So we looked for a hotel in which we could have at least some of them round us."

"They're lovely," I said. "That little bureau bookcase is a gem. And I think you chose very well when you came here. It's most comfortable."

There was a pause and Major Natterley said; "Oh yes. It's comfortable."

Jerrison brought in coffee and the Major charily made some mention of liqueurs. "Or do you prefer brandy?"

I chose an Armagnac and waited to find out why I had been invited.

"Yes, it's comfortable," said Major Natterley, "but just lately we have been a little undecided about it. We don't *want* to move . . ."

Dora Natterley turned to me and asked quite suddenly and point blank: "Have you noticed anything? Since you've been here, I mean, about this place?"

"Well . . ." I began.

"You have!" said Dora Natterley. "I knew it. It must be quite obvious to an outsider that things are not . . . normal here."

"I have noticed a certain air of constraint, perhaps. My friends who were here last year . . ."

"The Bellews. I remember them."

"Were so pleased with it. So am I, so far as that goes." By 'that' I suppose I meant comfort and food and all one asks of a guest house. "But I can't pretend that I haven't sensed something in the air."

"Ah," said Major Natterley, "that's just it. In the air. It's not something you can pin down."

"Mrs Derosse—whom incidentally I like enormously— seems to think it dates from Mrs Mallister's death." I remarked.

"In a way, perhaps," said Dora Natterley, "but we

couldn't help being aware of certain things that went on before that. We greatly dislike prying . . ."

"We don't want to know anything about other people's business," put in the Major.

"But we can't help being observant. Long before Mrs Mallister's death things were not what I would call right here. Lydia Mallister herself was a very difficult woman."

"We don't want to bore you with all this," said the Major suddenly to me.

"I assure you I'm not in the least bored," I replied truthfully.

"We never believe in troubling other people with our perplexities, but we could not resist asking a newcomer how these things appeared to her."

"Please go on. You were saying that Lydia Mallister was difficult."

"She had a very caustic tongue. We do not approve of slanderous remarks and some of those made by Lydia Mallister were in the worst of taste. She made no secret of her contempt for her husband and said in so many words that she believed he and Esmée Welton were . . ."

"Having an affair," I supplied when she hesitated.

"Thank you, yes, that is what she said. It is against our principles to discuss people in that way, but we could not help seeing what she meant. James Mallister was indiscreet before his wife's death and it has been positively scandalous since then. You cannot have failed to notice it."

"Yes, but I'm afraid I can't see anything remarkable in it. Mallister's not fifty and the girl is only about ten years younger than he is. They are both unattached. Why shouldn't they go about together? Or get married if they want to?"

"Oh, no reason, *now*. We are the last to show narrow-mindedness or intolerance. But we were speaking of Lydia

Mallister's lifetime. We do not dislike James Mallister or Esmée. Or, with one or two exceptions, anyone else in the house. We are trying to tell you how this very unpleasant state of things arose."

"Yes," I said with my first mild touch of impatience. "Well, there was Lydia Mallister, a woman with a sharp tongue, confined to her room upstairs, and there was her husband far too friendly with Esmée Welton downstairs! It's scarcely a unique situation."

"But the two were connected by the gossip that was carried to Lydia Mallister's room. We feel so strongly about this that we made a point of not visiting her. But there was no lack of ready informants and I daresay a good deal of exaggeration."

"We were given to understand," the Major took up the story, "that Bishop Grissell's sister was an old friend of Lydia Mallister's. It was even said they were at school together. We could not help noticing that she visited Mrs Mallister daily."

"And during the last months, Sonia Reid was scarcely less regular in her visits. Then Miss Godwin and Miss Grey would occasionally call on her in the afternoon."

"But all this is surely most natural?"

"Perhaps. But we felt it was the husband's duty to spend much of his time with his wife."

"And didn't he?"

"Not as much as he should have done."

"I gather that he has paid dearly for that."

"In money, you mean? Oh we never discuss money, Mrs Gort."

"You're very lucky. How do you manage?" There was a pained silence. "We never," said Dora at last, "discuss other people's money affairs."

"I see. I understand Mrs Mallister cut her husband out of her will."

"It's not a thing we would care to go into, but we have been told that he receives the very large sum for which her life was insured."

"Yes. That must have annoyed her," I said tactlessly. "She couldn't cut him out of that."

The Major wished to reprove my vulgarity with a change of subject, but could only think of offering me another drink, a thing he was most unwilling to do.

"Would you care for another brandy?" he ventured gingerly. He seemed surprised when I promptly said: "Yes, please."

"But there are other matters which have been forced on our notice," went on Dora Natterley. "Mrs Mallister was taking, on her doctor's prescription, some very powerful sleeping-pills called Dormatoze."

"Most invalids take one or another of these things," I said, "when they're confined to their rooms and have no exercise."

"That may be so. But a friend of ours who is a doctor tells us that an overdose of these to a woman in Lydia Mallister's condition would be fatal."

"Surely," I said, "an overdose of sleeping-pills can be fatal to anyone, whatever the condition. And, anyway, was there any question of this? Her doctor knew about them and gave a certificate."

"We understand he told Mr Mallister that his wife took one sleeping-pill each night. He said he was most careful to regulate this. He saw her every day, or every other day, and watched her supply. It is usual, I believe, with conscientious doctors to do so."

"Well then?"

"It is very distasteful to enter into these details, but we feel that as we live in the house we cannot entirely ignore them. There is a curious sequence to this. Dormatoze is not often prescribed and never legally sold without a prescription. Yet a fortnight after Mrs Mallister's death we were made aware that someone else in the house had a supply."

"Really? How was that?"

"I remained in bed one morning," said Dora Natterley, and I realized that she had used the singular pronoun at last. In the circumstances, perhaps, she could not very well do otherwise. "One of the women who works here, a Mrs Smithers, brought me some breakfast. I happened to mention that I had not slept well and she recommended me to take a sleeping-pill. 'Miss Reid has some,' she said, 'because I've seen them.' We do not care to question the servants, but I asked her, thinking that I might buy some, what Sonia Reid took. 'Dormatoze,' she said, 'the same as poor Mrs Mallister was taking. Only Miss Reid gets hers in London.' This so surprised me that I asked a question almost before I realized the impropriety of doing so. 'How do you know?' I said. 'Because it's on the box,' Mrs Smithers told me. 'From a chemist in Chelsea. I couldn't help noticing because I come from Battersea myself.'"

"I'm sorry," I told Dora Natterley, "but I can't see much in that."

"A girl like Sonia Reid taking sleeping-pills? She's in the very best of health. Besides, I asked her a few days later whether she ever had to take anything to help her to sleep. 'Never,' she told me. 'Sleep like a top.' So what were we to think?"

I said that did seem a little strange.

"We talked it over," went on Dora Natterley, and I realized that she was back to the conjugal 'we'. "We naturally had no wish to become involved in these matters, but we felt that this little detail might be disposed of at once by a word from Sonia Reid. We decided to tax her with it."

"We were most reluctant," put in the Major, "but the

40

household by then seemed so full of doubts and suspicions of all kinds that it would have been a relief to have this dismissed."

"And Sonia denied having any sleeping-pills?" I suggested.

"Worse than that," said Dora Natterley. "She became very angry and asked what on earth it was to do with us. We tried to explain that unfortunately we are all, much against our wills, caught up in these circumstances, but she became quite offensive. We said we had hoped she could dismiss our doubts immediately, but she said it was ridiculous to have any doubts on such a subject. Then we asked why, if she needed sleeping-pills, she had to go to London for them instead of getting them prescribed by Dr Cuffley. She said she happened to be in London when she wanted them. She had, in fact, spent a weekend in town a week or so before Mrs Mallister's death. We reminded her that she had told us she never took sleeping-pills and she called us impertinent to question her about it. You can see that we have cause to feel disturbed, can't you?"

"Not really, I'm afraid," I said as kindly as possible. "Unless you are seriously suggesting that Sonia Reid killed Mrs Mallister."

"We should never make such a suggestion," said Dora Natterley. "Never. It would be against all our principles. But we cannot help finding the circumstances questionable."

"Surely if you or anyone else in the house have reason to think that Mrs Mallister's death was not a natural one you have a remedy. You should go to the police."

"That we would certainly never do. We should find it quite unbearable to be involved in such a thing."

"But you say you are involved willy-nilly, Mrs Natterley."

"Not in police inquiries and a public scandal."

"I'm considered rather blunt," I told them both. "It seems to me a simple matter. Either you and the others believe that Lydia Mallister was murdered, or you have all allowed yourselves to get into a state of suspicion and doubt about nothing at all. If the first, you have an obvious duty. If the second, the sooner the whole thing is forgotten the better."

They both seemed to think this over.

"We find it so difficult to dismiss it from our minds," said Mrs Natterley at last. "Something is always happening to stir it up. Look at this evening, for instance, and the scene Sonia Reid made at dinner."

"Yes," I admitted, "that was unpleasant."

"Besides," said the Major. "It's not only the events of the past. You yourself have noticed it. What we cannot help feeling is that something is still going on, and perhaps even more is impending, too. It isn't at all comfortable."

"It's interesting," I could not help saying.

"But suppose it is also dangerous? If our very worst doubts are well-founded "—I let the curious phrase pass—" it seems likely that there is a murderer under this roof at this moment."

I considered that. "I hope you're not trying to frighten me, Major Natterley?" I said.

"Not in the least. We should never wish to do such a thing. But you do see the possibility?"

"I see that if Lydia Mallister was murdered—and I'm bound to say I have no reason as yet to think she was—it looks as though her murderer was someone who was then and is still in the house. No one has left since, I believe?"

"No one. We have made no study of crime, Mrs Gort, but it is commonly believed that a murderer too often finds himself under the necessity of striking again. Someone, perhaps, knows something which would be fatal to him if it were revealed, someone who may be unaware that he possesses any such information."

"That is a common gambit of crime fiction," I said, "but I don't know how often it happens in real life. Most double and treble murders seem to be the dreary repetitions of a sex maniac or of an utterly ruthless criminal obtaining money by a tried method."

"But there are cases, surely . . ."

"I can only call to mind one at the moment," I said. "The Birmingham Doctor Ruxton. He murdered his wife and found himself obliged to murder their servant who returned to the house unexpectedly and found him disposing of the body."

"I am sure there are many others. Frankly we cannot make up our minds whether to stay or not. If we leave, it might even look as though we had something to conceal."

"I suppose it might," I said politely, as though this had only now occurred to me.

"It is all very unpleasant. We have never had any experience of this kind before. We find it morbid. Yet we cannot help feeling a certain disquiet."

"We have found it a great relief to discuss the whole matter with you, Mrs Gort. We said today, that you would obviously have a level-headed view of it all. That is why we invited you to share our confidence."

"And your Armagnac," I said brightly. "I'm most grateful to you."

But when I reached my room I thought that both their Armagnac and their confidence had been shared sparingly.

5

It is three days since that conversation with the Natterleys and I know today that whatever 'it' is that they all discuss, I am now involved.

It's my own fault, really. I realized, as I made a certain remark, that I was throwing out a challenge, not to any individual but to fate. I had not really taken 'it' seriously. Good, gossiping Mrs Jerrison and those ridiculous Natterleys had failed to convince me that there was anything more in the house than a mild attack of mass hysteria. So during lunch, which gathers most of us together, I dropped my bombshell.

"I *always* keep a diary," I said.

Phiz exploded.

"Sheer sentimentality, diary-keeping," was her snorted comment. "Or exhibitionism."

"Not at all. My diary has very little in it about me."

"What is it about, then?"

"The people I meet, chiefly. Their affairs interest me far more than my own."

"Worse," said Phiz. "Mean to say after you leave us at night you go up to your room and write about us?"

"When there's anything to write about."

"Perhaps you would tell us," said the bishop rather haughtily, "whether you have found the trivialities of our life in this house worth a place in your diary?"

"Not the trivialities," I said, "except where they are significant. The realities. And, perhaps, the speculations."

The bishop grunted. I hoped it would recall to him a diary kept in Kenya or Kassala, Khartoum or Kafa Kumba, because I felt I had said more than was wise. But no. He seemed to take the matter too seriously for anec-dotes.

I also mentioned, as I see now foolishly, that I should not be in to dinner on the following evening. I told this to Mrs Derosse, but of course it was audible to everyone. I might have guessed what these two statements of mine would produce, but, as I say, I did not yet take the situation very seriously.

"Going up to town, Mrs Gort?" asked Esmée.

"No. Only to Northmere. I have some friends there."

"Going by car?" It was Steve Lawson who asked this.

"Yes. I've hired Woodhams."

I thought no more about these commonplace exchanges at the time and set out during the afternoon to visit Paul and Valerie, a young couple I have known for some years. Paul is an artist, Valerie very much a mother, and when I reached their place at tea-time I found that they were having one of their rare but devastating quarrels. I needn't go into that—it concerned the children; Paul's work; Valerie's being *tied* to the house like a *slave*; Paul not having a moment's peace in which to think; Valerie's friends being *insulted* when they came to see her; Paul being unable to suffer fools; Valerie thanking God that she could or she would have left long ago; Paul remember-ing someone called Michael and Valerie wanting to know what about a certain Gloria. It was quite evident that they would enjoy this better if left to themselves and that it would be protracted by the presence of a third person. If I left them to reach a climax of bitterness and recrimi-nation at about ten o'clock that evening, they would be in bed, in tears, and in one another's arms by eleven. But, if I stayed, it would go on till they were too tired for reconciliation. So I made an excuse and by half-past six was approaching Cat's Cradle.

I stopped the chauffeur in the road beyond the drive

and walked up to the front door, which is kept open. I met no one and thought with some amusement that the evening's 'changing' had begun.

I had been thinking, on my way back from Northmere, about the Natterleys' 'strike again' theory, which had seemed to me at the time merely melodramatic. Yet, I remembered, there is nothing quite as dangerous as a creature cornered and afraid. If it was true that there had been a murder here, it was also true, as I had admitted, that it was almost certainly by someone in the house. To carry the hypothesis farther, if someone else was the only person with information—consciously or not—which would incriminate the culprit, then it was quite logical to expect him or her, given the opportunity, to eliminate the one who knew too much. But there were several conditions attached to this. The murderer wouldn't do it unless the proof was clear and definite and had not already been passed on. To hasten the death of a woman who could not in any case live long might be the act of someone cowardly and desperate, but not by nature homicidal. To plan and carry out the death of someone who happened to have incriminating knowledge was a different and perhaps more inhuman crime.

I could at a pinch believe that any one of the guests at Cat's Cradle was capable, with sufficient motive, of the first. But I could not imagine any of them guilty of the second. All the same I felt a certain relief, I will admit, that I had not been here at the time of Mrs Mallister's death and could not be in possession of any fatal piece of evidence.

Then I opened the door of my room. My sensations during the next few moments were curious, a mixture of choking fear and resolution to remain calm. I knew at once that someone was there. Just as people who are unfortunate enough to be allergic to cats instantly sense the presence of one in a room, wherever it may be hidden, so I knew immediately that someone concealed was watching me. There was no light as I opened the door and I switched it on at once. How did I know someone was there? There was no extraneous scent, either of tobacco or perfume. Nothing was out of place.

It seemed to me that my life depended on my remaining quite cool. If I discovered the identity of my visitor, it would put me in extreme danger, not perhaps immediately but thereafter. This was nonsense, of course, because, if I immediately roused the house, everyone would know who was in my room and I should not possess secret and dangerous knowledge. But one does not think like that. I felt only that I must not, on any account, know who was there, and the important thing was not to reveal that I had the smallest awareness of any presence but my own. Yet I longed more than I can say to walk straight out to the landing and scream at the top of my voice.

This is perhaps what I should have done, for then the whole household would have come. But though I kept my head pretty well I was not capable of acting except in the way I had determined. I took off my hat and gloves, smoothed my hair, and slowly, as casually as I could, crossed to the door and, switching off the light, went out. I should have liked to wash, but the bathroom door was ajar and this was one of the places in which someone could quickly have hidden on my approach.

I did not hesitate on the landing, but went straight downstairs to find myself alone in the lounge. I was feeling distinctly jittery and rang the bell. Before Jerrison appeared, however, I managed to pick up a newspaper and appeared quite calm as I asked for a large whisky-and-soda.

Slowly the sheer funk I had felt began to give way to

curiosity. I realized that, if I knew who was in my bedroom, I should almost certainly know the answer to everything that was perplexing me in this house. There could only be one reason for the visit—my diary. Someone was anxious to find out whether anything that a newcomer to the house might have realized or been told was dangerous. Someone was sufficiently anxious to take the risk of being seen entering or leaving my room. I suppose I am an excessively inquisitive person. I was almost inquisitive enough to wish that I had boldly looked into the two or three possible hiding-places. But not quite. For there could be no doubt now that there was danger here. 'Mortal danger', I said to myself, not liking the words.

Just then the bishop entered. I at once had an idea. He would not make the same mistake as I had. Mine had been failure to realize in time that, if I made a big scene and everyone knew at once who was in my room, I should be no more in danger than anyone else. If the bishop found someone there, he would reveal it and it would not implicate him, for the whole house would know. As for any immediate danger, he could certainly take care of himself. He had not coped with cannibals and crocodiles for nothing.

"I wonder if I know you well enough to ask you a small favour?" I said as sweetly as I could.

He did not look pleased, but said: "Of course, Mrs Gort."

"I am absolutely dead beat," I said. "I have been over to Northmere and back and for some reason it has tired me out. I went up to my room when I came in and left my glasses there. May I impose on your kindness?"

He looked positively relieved. Perhaps he had thought I wanted to borrow money.

"I should be delighted," he said.

48

"I don't know where they are. The bathroom perhaps. I put them down in the oddest places. I'm so sorry to trouble you."

He looked at me fixedly for a moment and I felt uncomfortable. Did he know I was lying? Or was he remembering someone who had lost his binoculars in Nairobi or Nigeria? At all events he went.

I realized that it was unlikely that my visitor would have remained there, but there was just a chance that, thinking I would not return before dinner, whoever it was had stayed to read my diary, which was lying on the writing-table. In any case, I wanted to be sure that the room was now clear of that hidden presence.

The other guests had begun to gather before the bishop returned, full of apologies because, although he had looked *everywhere*, he said, he had failed to find my glasses. This was scarcely to be wondered at, since they were safely in my bag.

Jerrison was in the lounge while the bishop made his report and I remembered guiltily that he had seen me wearing my glasses to read the paper when he had brought me my whisky-and-soda. He said nothing, however, and, after thanking the bishop profusely, I said I should have to go and look for myself, because I cannot see to eat without them. As I left the room, I heard Phiz Grissell say something sharp about women who were always losing things.

This time I carefully locked the door on the inside and took my time in getting ready. I was pleased to find that the incident had not left any unpleasant traces in the room or its atmosphere. I had liked the room since I first saw it and I liked it still, but I resolved to keep the door locked in future. I rejoined the others in the lounge. They turned as I came in and I thought there was expectancy or perhaps anxiety among them. Since presumably someone in the room had been my visitor, I realized the necessity of lying convincingly.

" *Where* do you think they were? " I said, showing my glasses to the astonished bishop. " I really must be getting rather dotty! I had put them under my pillow as I always do before getting into bed. No wonder you could not find them! "

I beamed round on everybody but, if I expected to see any signs of disquiet, I was mistaken. The Gee-Gees nodded politely but most of the others looked bored, as well they might be.

There was a quarter of an hour to pass before the second gong and I took a seat in the farthest corner of the lounge and looked, I hoped, a benevolent old lady pleased and amused by the antics of her juniors.

Nobody seemed quite natural. Nobody seemed, for that matter, to be what he was supposed to be. Steve Lawson was not, I thought as I looked at his hard mouth and troubled eyes, a carefree playboy with a large income. James Mallister was by no means a heartbroken widower, and Esmée beside him looked far too clever and expensively dressed and altogether sophisticated to be the manageress of a local shop. Miss Godwin and Miss Grey were certainly spinsterish in appearance and one could well believe they had spent much of their lives teaching in school, but weren't they rather too much in character to be natural? Or was it merely their presence in this house which made me think this? And the Natterleys— afraid to stay, they said, because they scented danger, and afraid to leave because it might look as though they had something to conceal. Even the bishop seemed curiously unepiscopal as he swallowed a third sherry. I supposed he must be what he said he was and Phiz could scarcely be anything else, but I thought as I watched them that there was something very odd about the pair.

The only person who was almost blatantly herself was Sonia Reid. Attractive, sensual, intelligent, she could only be, as I divined on my first evening, the *femme fatale* of the whole ménage.

As I watched them all, so unnatural, so determined to make light conversation while their thoughts were anything but light, I decided that I had been quite wrong this evening in my analysis. I had thought then that, whereas any of these people might have hastened the death of Lydia Mallister, none of them, so far as I could imagine, was capable of a cold-blooded murder to conceal his crime. I had missed a very important thing—the change in the atmosphere of the house. When Lydia Mallister died they were, I believed, a reasonably contented ordinary collection of people. Indeed, my friends the Bellews, who had stayed here only a few months ago, described it as a happy place. Murder in such a household would be a calculated, resolute crime by someone born to such an act. Murder in this seething atmosphere of suspicion and intrigue might almost be an act of despair.

"You came home earlier than you intended then, Mrs Gort?"

It was Esmée Welton who had taken a seat beside me.

"Yes. I found my friends in the middle of a big conjugal row and left them to it."

Esmée smiled. "So you preferred the intrigues of Cat's Cradle to their open warfare?"

"Yes."

"We must seem an unholy lot to you."

She seemed to be asking for it, so I decided to let her have it in my best direct manner.

"Tell me, Miss Welton," I said. "Do *you* believe Lydia Mallister was murdered?"

Her reaction was a complete surprise. Moreover I am certain that it was natural and genuine.

"*Murdered?*" she said at once, as though of all possibilities this had certainly never occurred to her. "What a monstrous idea! Of course she wasn't murdered!"

I was shaken. "I am only repeating something that has been more than once suggested to me," I said apologetically.

"Oh!" She seemed quite distressed by the idea. "Who could possibly think such a thing? There has never been any question . . ." She looked pale and I saw that her knuckles were white as she clasped her hands.

"Now I've made you think me a tiresome old alarmist," I said. "But you must admit there is a lot of talk in this house."

"Yes, but not *murder*. No one has ever suggested that."

"I'm sorry if I've said something to upset you."

She managed to gain control of herself. "I do know that beastly things are said by people, but I never knew anyone could go as far as that. I don't mean you, Mrs Gort. Someone must have told you that. *Please* don't take any notice of it."

"The whole thing is no business of mine," I said, "whatever 'the whole thing' may be. I came here to work. I was told it was the sort of place in which one could work."

"It used to be," said Esmée rather sadly.

"I'm sure it will be again. All this will be forgotten very soon." She gave me a little smile, but it did not seem to imply agreement. "I should like to come and see you at your shop one day. I'm told you have such nice things and I'm in need of a lot."

"Do," she said absently. "Yes, please do. I shall look forward to it."

We went in to dinner.

6

NEXT morning I decided to have a talk with Mrs Derosse. To be candid, I was thinking of leaving. Looking back on it now, it seems almost incredible that at that point I could have packed up and gone with no difficulty and never have been involved in all that followed. I still cannot imagine why I hesitated. Perhaps it was the reassurances, equivocal though they were, of Mrs Derosse.

"I know what you're going to say, Mrs Gort," she began at once.

I always find that statement a little irritating. "Then I needn't trouble to say it," I replied.

"You find the atmosphere disagreeable and you want to give up your room."

"I hadn't quite decided about giving up my room. but I *do* find the atmosphere, not disagreeable so much as disturbing. I'm not getting my work done."

"I was afraid of that. What is it, Mrs Gort? I would be grateful if you would tell me what you feel. You are the only one who wasn't here at the time of Mrs Mallister's death and it's since then that this change has come about."

"It's hard to say. At first I thought it was a psychological thing and the idea really rather interested me. How some kind of vague suspicion, with no foundation at all perhaps, could start in a little community like this, then grow and grow till it involved everyone and made everything appear rather sinister. How people who had seemed quite commonplace before began to take on a strangeness and ugliness; how actions which nobody previously would have noticed seemed to have some occult significance. How all this, fed by talk and perhaps some natural antipathies, grew till it was an obsession. That was my first idea."

"And now?"

"Now I'm not so sure that it has no foundation."

"You mean . . . something to do with Mrs Mallister?"

"Let's not beat about the bush, Mrs Derosse. There are a number of people in this house who believe that Lydia Mallister did not die naturally."

"But Dr Cuffley . . ."

"I'm not giving any opinion as to what happened. I'm only saying what is being thought. And it goes further than that. It has been suggested to me that something else very unpleasant may come out of this. In other words, if there is any truth in the idea, then we have someone among us with—to put it mildly—a very guilty conscience and a number of secrets to keep at all costs. Such a person could be dangerous."

"Yes," said Mrs Derosse with a little sigh of resignation. "I realize all that." She hesitated, then brought out a statement by which, it was clear, she believed she had answered everything. "I have asked my niece to come and stay," she announced.

It was surprising in itself, and surprising in that Mrs Derosse, saying it, seemed to think she had solved every problem.

"Your niece?"

"I have only one, Christine. When you meet her, Mrs Gort, you will understand why I feel such confidence. She will know at once what to do about all this. She's so very brave and competent. She is also extremely shrewd. I believe that within a week of her arrival this nasty business will be over."

"But *how*?"

"I don't know. But I trust Christine. It was she who made me buy this house and until now I have been very successful here. She made me get rid of the Lampards, a couple of guests I had who were causing endless trouble though I did not realize it. She found the Jerrisons, who have been wonderful. She will get at the truth of this in no time and tell me what to do."

"She must be a remarkable young woman."

"She is, Mrs Gort."

I smiled. "At any rate I must stay and meet her," I said. "When does she arrive?"

"On Thursday. I'm very glad you're staying. It would be dreadful if people felt they had to leave here because of all this."

"I'm rather surprised, frankly, that none of your residents have done so—the bishop and his sister, for instance."

"Miss Grissell received a very large legacy from Mrs Mallister," pointed out Mrs Derosse.

"I don't see why that should make her stay."

"It would look bad for them to leave."

With that phrase she explained everything. I knew the power of 'it would look bad' among conventional people.

"Or the Natterleys," I suggested.

"Perhaps they feel the same. At any rate, when Christine comes, I think things will soon be as they used to be. I always have a waiting-list of people anxious to live here, you know."

"I'm not surprised. It is very comfortable."

"Your room was vacant because for the last six months Mr Mallister occupied it. His wife preferred to be alone. After her death he moved back to the room they had shared, which is the best in the house."

"I see. Well, I hope your niece is successful in laying this ghost, or whatever it is. I think the most unpleasant aspect of it is that someone takes it seriously enough to enter your guests' rooms when they are not there."

"Oh, you mean what Sonia Reid said the other night. But she's always been a rather excitable girl."

"I don't mean only that." I hesitated. I had told no one about my own visitor and had intended not to do so. But I wanted a Yale lock put on my door in order not to carry about the heavy key of the mortice lock. Also I knew that in houses like this the locks were often identical and there might be other keys to fit mine.

"What do you mean, Mrs Gort?" asked Mrs Derosse anxiously.

"Last night when I returned from Northmere I found someone in my room."

Mrs Derosse looked startled, but asked no question.

"I don't know who it was. I came away at once."

"Are you *sure*?"

"Oh, absolutely. One can sense a human presence in a room."

"Why didn't you tell me?"

"I told no one and I wish no one to be told now. But I would be glad if you would have a Yale lock put on my door, today if possible."

"Yes. I certainly will. Oh dear, I wish I had known! And I wish Christine could come before Thursday!"

It was not in fact until the Friday morning that Mrs Derosse's niece arrived. She drove up in a sports car before lunch. I saw the arrival from my window and certainly her swift, decisive driving and brisk yet graceful movements did look like confidence. She wore a pale-grey coat and skirt and one of those very smart hats which look as though they have been snatched from a peg and pulled on like a man's hat, but of course have been nothing of the sort. Even before I saw her face, I liked the look of her.

I soon found I was the only person in the house unacquainted with her. She called the serious-looking Jerrison 'Jerry' and seemed popular with him and his wife. She was at once charming and exhilarating to me.

She was older than I had thought when I saw her alight—perhaps thirty-three or -four. Dark hair and large, laughing eyes, yet a somewhat cheeky profile which saved her from leaving any suggestion of one of those noble Roman faces which always mean a boring woman. We were alone in the lounge for a time, Mrs Derosse having, deliberately I thought, left us together.

"Let's have a drink," she said at once. "I'll tell Jerry. What would you like?"

It was the first time in that house anyone had used those very ordinary words and I was pleased.

"Now what's it all about?" she asked.

"Nothing—or everything. Either there has been a murder here or all your aunt's guests have worked themselves to a point not far from hysteria over nothing at all."

"What do you think?"

"Your aunt asked me that. I would say there is sufficient to make some of them very frightened. Moreover, there have been one or two nasty little things like room-searching."

"You don't think it could be something else? Nothing to do with Lydia Mallister at all?"

"Frankly that hadn't occurred to me. Everyone seems to go back to Lydia Mallister's death as a matter of course."

"A red herring, perhaps?"

"It's possible, I suppose. Did you know her?"

"Yes. Small, mean and vain. She could switch on a sort of wan charm when she liked and was intelligent and musical. I would say she would go to almost any length to do something thoroughly malicious."

"Did she know she had to die?"

"Oh yes. She soon got that out of the specialists and, to do her justice, she faced it with courage. She knew almost to the day. Why? What are you thinking?"

"It was your saying that she would go to almost any length to be malicious. Do you think that, if she knew she was dying, she was capable of doing something which would make it look as though she had been murdered? Out of spite, I mean?"

Christine smiled.

"A brilliant idea. I would say it was possible but only if it involved James Mallister, and it couldn't very well do that. He was in hospital. Perhaps your ingenious mind is working out something about that? No, no. He really was in hospital. My aunt has checked on it. He couldn't have got out or anything. My aunt saw the night nurse. Besides, he was far too ill. No, I'm afraid your idea is out. She hated her husband with all the venom she had got, but no one else like that."

"What about Esmée Welton?"

Again Christine gave me that very full smile. "Oh, it wasn't that kind of hatred. I don't think she cared a damn about James and Esmée having an affair, or whatever they were having. No, she hated James for himself, for having married her and seen her health decline, for being a cheerful and good-natured man and for not being as ill as she was. See what I mean?"

"Whom else did she dislike?"

"Pretty well everyone except Phiz. But she only had one hate in her life, just as other people only have one love. That was for James. It was quite terrifyingly intense."

"Did he know it?"

"Not fully. He used to say he was afraid he got on her nerves. I don't think he felt anything much for her, except a sort of mild wonder and admiration at her courage."

Presently she said: "I hear you were thinking of leaving?"

"I was, yes. I've got some work to do."

"I hope you won't go. You're the only person I can talk to. I'm devoted to my aunt, but she's really in such a state over this that she can't discuss it sensibly."

"What do you intend to do?" I asked.

"Find out what it's all about. I'm no detective, but I've got some common sense, which is all that's needed here. I've had to come to my aunt's rescue before."

"You seem very confident."

"I am. I'll soon find out who's playing monkey-tricks and have them out of the place in a flash. We can't have this."

"You don't think there's any danger in the situation?"

To my surprise she did not dismiss this. "I don't know," she said. "I shall have to *feel* that."

"Abject fear is always dangerous," I said rather pompously.

"Beast at bay? Yes, I know. I suppose the most ordinary person could do something desperate and violent out of fear. What do you think of the Gee-Gees?"

"I scarcely know them."

"I've always thought them rather pets, but then I've always quite liked everyone at Cat's Cradle. In different ways, of course. Even Lydia Mallister."

We were interrupted there by Mrs Derosse's return and soon afterwards those guests who were lunching in the house began to gather.

The idea that Christine had brought sunlight into the house has been borne out by the weather, which has suddenly turned Mediterranean. After a patchy summer with a July that I could only call chilly, it seems that August will go out in placid splendour. The winds round this house on a headland have been strong and various until

59

now, but they seem to have dropped in deference to the golden sunlight. I am very pleased, of course, and amused by the coincidence of this coming at the time of Christine's arrival, so that Miss Godwin and Miss Grey can both say: "You've brought the fine weather with you, anyhow!"

But this evening something happened which I disliked very much. I overheard a conversation. Only once or twice in my life has this happened to me by accident and I have never, needless to say, sought deliberately to overhear.

It was so warm and still that after dinner I went into the garden, which is on the more sheltered side of the house and in weather like this is delightful. I must say that Mrs Derosse is lucky in her employees, for Smithers the gardener seems as good as the Jerrisons. There was plenty of starlight and a thin new moon—would it be a harvest moon?—but the light was not sufficient to allow me to do anything but just sit quietly. I had almost dropped off to sleep when I heard voices.

For a moment I did not know whose they were or just where they were coming from. They were disembodied voices, as it were, sadly calling across the night. Then I realized that they were rising to me from the terrace below. On this, the south side of the house, the garden goes down in terraces almost to the beach. The speakers' heads were not twenty feet from mine but, because they were lower and there was a rocky slope rising from where they stood, they had the illusion of being very much alone. Few people know how clearly voices carry upwards on a still night.

I recognized them after a moment—Steve Lawson and Sonia Reid.

"Won't listen," she was saying. "Doesn't believe I've got it and anyway it's too late now."

"But it's not. It's never too late. We can prove they knew."

"I said that. Wants to see it."

"Bluffing . . . You've *got* to get it, do you hear? You've damn well got to! If not . . ."

A little of Sonia's spirit seemed to return. "If not, *what*?" she asked defiantly.

"If not, you know what I shall do."

"You wouldn't. I know you wouldn't. I'm not afraid of that."

"I damn well would! You've got to get it and get it at once . . ."

This, I thought, is where I came in. How should I take myself out of earshot? They were coming up the steps to where I was sitting and if I stood up and walked away they would see me. I thought the best thing was to greet them as soon as they came in sight as though it was the first I knew.

"Hullo! " I said, "you two popped up like someone from the underworld. Is there a way right down to the beach there?"

Sonia kept her head. "Hullo, Mrs Gort! Yes, we've been down to the bay. No moonlight bathing, though. That's an over-rated pleasure if ever there was one."

"How long have you been sitting here?" asked Steve Lawson, quite pleasantly but with a hint of anxiety in his voice.

"Only a few minutes," I said, "and I'm going in now. But it *is* lovely tonight, isn't it? Let's all go in and have a nightcap."

Actually I drink very little, but I think I have a reputation at Cat's Cradle for liking it more than an old lady should. Anyway, they both seemed quite pleased to join me, relieved that I had apparently overheard nothing of their somewhat cryptic conversation.

Who, I wondered when I was in my room later, wouldn't listen? And what were the two 'its'? The 'it' which someone didn't believe Sonia had, and the 'it' which she must at all costs get?

7

REALLY, the atmosphere in this house grows more and more like the threatening stillness which comes before a thunderstorm. It's quite uncanny. Not the weather—the weather is as gorgeous as ever, and we're all saying we've never known so many hours of sunshine in England. No, it's the atmosphere *in* the house. No one seems unaffected by it.

After lunch today I found myself alone in the garden with the bishop and his sister. I ought to have gone up to my room at once and started to work, but it was so pleasant in the deckchair on the lawn which forms the highest terrace that I foolishly stayed too long and saw the two tall figures bearing down on me. If it was to be only reminiscences of Nairobi or Natal, Ngoundere or Niagara, I could doze in peace but there was a look in their eyes which suggested that their approach was purposeful and that I was in for something more immediate than Mother Hubbards or big game. I was right.

"Settling down, Mrs Gort?" boomed the bishop. "Find you can work here?"

"Splendidly, thank you," I said disobligingly.

This seemed to nonplus him somewhat. "Don't find too many distractions?" he tried.

"None. That's why I chose Cat's Cradle."

"That's why *we* chose it originally, wasn't it, Phiz my dear?"

"It *was*," said Phiz. She has a trick of drawing in her breath sharply and nasally after voicing her monosyllables. It has the effect of a snort.

"No longer, I fear," said the bishop. "No longer a peaceful little haven, unfortunately. After a vigorous and I hope fruitful life, we found in this remote place the very repose we had always wanted. 'Port after stormy seas, ease after war', you know. Not once but many times as we were paddled up the crocodile-infested rivers of Madagascar in our frail canoes, I remarked to my sister that one day we would return to England and settle down for the evening of our days. At last the time came and we did so. Then what happened?"

The question was clearly rhetorical but Phiz could not resist it. "Murder!" she said and snorted vigorously.

"I would not go as far as to say that," returned the bishop judiciously, "but our old friend Lydia Mallister died in what we cannot help thinking ambiguous circumstances. Her life, it is true, had been despaired of by the doctors, though not by us. We have seen far too many miraculous recoveries in far places to despair of one here, with all medical science to aid it."

"Remember Mwomba?" asked Phiz with something intended for a smile on her equine face.

"A case in point!" said the bishop enthusiastically. "Mwomba-Mwomba was a tribal chief in my diocese . . ."

"And he recovered?" I asked, looking impressed, but at the same time neatly curtailing several minutes of missionary narrative.

"He did, though his case was considered quite as hopeless as that of Lydia Mallister. Mind you"—he raised a bristly forefinger—"I do not say that Lydia would have mended completely. But I firmly believe she might have been alive today."

"Then why isn't she?" I asked innocently.

"Ah," said the bishop, throwing into the interjection such occult significance that I was startled.

"That's the point," said Phiz.

"You knew her well?"

"School chums," said Phiz loudly. "Ragged old Holly together—Miss Hollington, games mistress. Lyddy was a sport."

I had not previously heard her speak at such length and thought this betokened some deep sentiment or emotion.

"We were not, however," the bishop pontificated, "on such intimate terms with the man she married. We have never, to be frank, felt much confidence in Mallister."

"Stinker!" put in Phiz, reverting to her normal curtness.

"My sister, as you will observe, Mrs Gort, is apt to be a mite . . . categorical. But there certainly has always seemed to us to be something unhealthy about Mallister."

I felt it was time to make some contribution to this friendly chatter. "I must say he looks the picture of health to me," I said.

"Physically, doubtless. But I am not a blind believer in the tag *mens sana in corpore sano*. I have known too many excessively unhealthy minds in patently healthy bodies for that. I remember, for instance, a man in Durban"—or was it Dondo or Dar-es-Salaam?—"a powerful fellow in the pink of condition . . ."

"But with a nasty mind?" I interpolated briskly. "Yet I wouldn't say that of Mallister. I have spoken to him several times and he seems to be a very normal creature."

It occurred to me at that moment that, with these two and others in the house, Mallister would have had a poor chance if he had not been absent at the time of his wife's death.

"Normal? Man's a monster!" shouted Phiz.

"You see, Mrs Gort, our affection for our old friend Lydia Mallister makes us perhaps too keenly observant. We cannot help seeing that there is an association of sorts between him and the young woman Esmée Welton."

"You don't need to be keenly observant to see that," I told them. "I saw it my first day in the house. But what about it? They're both free agents."

"You saw it at once, did you?" said the bishop. "That's highly significant."

"I told you," said Phiz to her brother. "They're quite shameless."

"It is not the present situation which gives us concern," explained the bishop patiently. "They are, as you say, free agents. But this had started while our poor Lydia was still alive."

"Did she mind?" I asked innocently.

"I beg your pardon?"

I repeated my question.

"What would *you* feel?" asked Phiz sharply. "Husband running around with another woman."

"It would depend on the husband," I pointed out reasonably.

This seemed to baffle them and I saw them exchange glances. The bishop then began from a new angle.

"We are not, I hope, intolerant or narrow-minded people. We have seen too much of the world and its ways for that. When I first took up my ministry to the people of the Comorro Islands I found . . ."

"Terrible," I said quickly. "But this is England."

"I was about to demonstrate that we have seen and heard too much to be stuffy. But in this case we felt our broad-mindedness was stretched to the utmost."

"It was flagrant," said Phiz.

Yet, I thought, it had not been without advantage to Miss Grissell. Perhaps this was an unkind and unworthy thought, but the pomposity of the bishop and the growls of his sister were not easy to bear.

"You dislike Mallister," I said. "All right. We are all entitled to our likes and dislikes. But you can scarcely connect Mallister with what you call the ambiguity about his wife's death. He had been in hospital for some weeks when it happened. Fortunately for him, in the light of subsequent gossip, he wasn't even in the house."

"No, but Esmée Welton was," said Phiz.

This left a very nasty silence.

"Are you really suggesting . . ." I began, but this time it was I who was interrupted by the bishop. "We are suggesting nothing," he said. "Far be it from me to add to the suspicions and suggestions already rife. No one wishes more that all his doubts could be dissolved, but the memory of our old friend puts us under certain obligations. It has been rumoured that since the obstacle of Mallister's married state has been removed by Lydia's death, the two of them, Mallister and Esmée Welton, are contemplating matrimony. We feel that, before that happens, further investigations should be made. I would have been failing in my duty if I had not pointed out to the authorities that there were those of us here who were far from satisfied with the facts that have so far emerged."

"The authorities?" I asked.

"I have communicated with the Chief Constable," said the bishop. "Colonel Lyle de Lisle De lisle L'Isle."

"An acquaintance of yours?"

"Rather more than that. Lie Low, as he was called in the service, has been a friend of mine since our days in Bulawayo"—or was it Basutoland or Bloemfontein?—

"and what days they were! I remember on one occasion . . ."

"How very fortunate that he is now the Chief Constable here!" I said crisply. "And what does he think of this matter?"

"Ah, that I cannot tell you. The police here as in other parts of the world must preserve a discreet silence about their inner thoughts. But at least he is in possession of what few facts are known to us. What steps he will order we cannot say, but remembering my friend Lie Low and his love of thoroughness, I should not be surprised if they were exhumation and a post-mortem."

"In other words, you think Lydia Mallister was poisoned?"

"It is not for us . . ." began the bishop, but his sister cut in: "Of course she was!"

I was beginning to understand how people had been convicted of crimes through local gossip and suspicion.

"I wonder," I said, "why you tell me all this?"

"I feel that, as an arrival here after the main events, you should be put in the picture," said the bishop. "I wish to make no secret of the fact that I have written to Colonel L'Isle."

"Then let me make my position clear," I said. "I do not deny that since I came here my curiosity has been aroused. I should not be human if it hadn't. But not by the death of Lydia Mallister. I see no reason to think that anything but natural. What has intrigued me is the spectacle of all the guests and staff working themselves up to a state of suspicion and even fear. Into this I will not be drawn."

I thought that put the matter pretty strongly and would settle both the bishop and his formidable sister, but I had underestimated them. They rose together as if by pre-arrangement and stood over me.

"I don't think you will be able to avoid it," said the bishop. "If you remain here, that is. I don't think anyone in the house will be able to avoid it." They moved away and I was left to think over *that*.

But that conversation, curious as its implications were, was nothing to what happened later today. I am still bewildered by the unexpectedness of it.

Since I came here I have had very little to do with Sonia Reid. Except for the occasion on which I accidentally overheard her conversation with Steve Lawson we have scarcely exchanged a word beyond the daily civilities. What, indeed, should we have in common? She is one of those passionate people who seem to throw a tremendous amount into the mere business of living and I must appear to be a rather quiet old party. Yet this evening, after dinner, she got me alone for a moment. " Mrs Gort," she whispered quickly. " Could I possibly ask a favour of you? It's only that I would like to talk with you."

She seemed so intense that I deliberately treated this lightly. " Of course," I said.

" I mean a private talk. Could I come to your room? "

" Yes, certainly, if you like," I said, " though I don't see why we shouldn't sit in the garden."

" No, please. I don't want anyone to see us talking. You'll understand why when I tell you."

" But if you were seen coming to my room . . ."

" I shan't be. I have the room in the tower, as they call it, and use the bathroom on your floor. So no one would be surprised to meet me in the corridor."

All this was said hurriedly and she seemed to be looking about her as though afraid someone would observe even this brief exchange.

" What time may I come? " Her voice was pleading.

" I usually go up about eleven and read or write for a

time before going to bed. Come as soon as possible after I go up."

She nodded and hurried away.

I certainly could not complain of being left out, I reflected. Everyone seemed anxious to confide in me. Everyone except Miss Godwin and Miss Grey, and perhaps they had nothing to confide.

I joined them on the terrace and we chatted rather feebly for a time, for I was absent-minded, wondering what on earth I was going to hear from Sonia, and they quietly continued with their needlework. I remembered Mrs Jerrison's story about Miss Godwin's one unexpected outbreak but, as they sat there, they looked complacent and assured, the last people to have ugly suspicions of their fellows.

We chatted of the weather, of course—it was hard to do otherwise in that late un-English heat wave—then relapsed into comfortable silence. Their calm made me feel that perhaps after all the whole thing was preposterous and I ought never to have listened to Mrs Jerrison or anyone else. While these two very ordinary old ladies could remain in the house coolly continuing to change their books at the lending library and do their needlework, oblivious of or indifferent to the suspicions around them, there could not be much wrong.

Then Miss Godwin gave me a look as keen as the needle she was using. "I saw the Grissells talking to you this afternoon," she said.

It was a relief to hear her use the first person singular. The 'we' of Natterleys and Grissells always seemed somewhat unnatural to me. But there was no mistaking the sharpness in her voice.

"Yes," I said blandly. "At least the bishop talked. His sister as you know only puts in a word now and again."

"It's quite enough," said Miss Godwin. "I suppose they told you of their suspicions about Lydia Mallister."

"Yes, but everyone seems to do that, except you and Miss Grey. It's a relief to be with you."

The needles never stopped.

"I never discuss it," said Miss Godwin.

"How calm the sea is tonight!" put in Miss Grey, speaking for the first time since I had joined them.

When at last I went up to my room it was little more than half past ten but in a few minutes there was a gentle knock on the door. I did not call 'come in' but went across and opened it. Sonia Reid stood there and with a hurried smile quickly entered. I pointed to a chair and we sat facing one another. She did not seem in the least nervous or embarrassed, but had an almost mischievous smile on her face, as though she wanted me to join her in playing a practical joke.

"You must think this very odd of me," she began.

"I've ceased to think anything odd," I told her.

She smiled broadly. "I know. We must all seem rather peculiar to you. I want to tell you something."

Looking at her I realized that there was something very ruthless about this young woman. I felt it had cost her a great effort to come to me, but that it was part of a course of action on which she was utterly determined. "Before you do so," I said gently, "may I ask why you should have chosen me? There must surely be someone you know better in whom you can confide."

"That's just it," she said. "They were all here. They are all concerned in this thing, and you are not."

"They weren't all here," I pointed out. "Why don't you go to Christine Derosse? She has just arrived and I'm sure she's more able to cope with things than I am."

She shook her head vigorously. "Oh no!" she said. "She doesn't like me and I wouldn't trust her. Besides, it is not after all very much that I want to ask you. Just to look after something for me for a few days."

" Something? "

" Well, an envelope."

" An empty envelope? "

" Of course not, Mrs Gort." She could smile charmingly when she liked. " It has a . . . paper in it."

" A letter? "

" A sort of letter."

" But, my dear girl, why on earth don't you put it in your bank for safe keeping? Even with all the safe-blowing and bank raids we're having nowadays, surely a bank is the safest place for a valuable document? "

" There are two reasons, as a matter of fact. But the chief one is that I need this document here in the house."

" Then hide it in your room."

" I have. But I never feel it's safe. My room's been searched twice."

" You may be surprised to know that my room has been searched, too."

'Surprised' was mild. She positively goggled at me. " Yours? But why? "

" I supposed that it was because I foolishly admitted keeping a diary."

She stared at me, seeming to consider this. " Was your diary taken? "

" No. But it may have been read. I've had a Yale lock put on the door now."

" Then *do* take this—if it's only for tonight." She opened her bag and was about to take out a thickly sealed envelope. But as she did so I was able to observe that her bag held two of these and they looked identical.

" Why tonight? " I asked firmly.

" Because . . . Oh, I don't know. I have a feeling . . ."

" You know, Miss Reid, what you are asking me is quite

71

impossible. I couldn't look after a document the nature of which I don't know. And you admit that someone wants to get hold of it."

She was evidently determined to try everything. Tears were in her large eyes. "I thought you would help me."

"How can I when I don't know what I am helping you to do? Let's be frank and say what it *looks* like."

"What does it look like?"

"Blackmail," I said, and let the word hang in the air.

She grew neither indignant nor hysterical. "You mean you think this document contains evidence against someone?"

"Could be," I said relentlessly.

"Perhaps you think it contains evidence that Lydia Mallister was murdered?" There was a strange, rather dangerous calm in her voice now.

"Look at it from my point of view. Remember what I have seen and heard in this house about Lydia Mallister's death. It's not an unreasonable conclusion to draw, is it?"

"Mrs Gort, I swear it isn't that. You must believe me. The envelope I ask you to keep contains a document, yes, but it contains no evidence that Lydia Mallister was murdered."

"You promise that?"

"I'll swear to it. Oh, please keep this for me."

For a moment I hesitated, then fortunately refused. "I'm sorry. I could not possibly do that."

Suddenly she seemed to give way, to realize that it was hopeless. She stood up. "You won't tell anyone I asked you?"

"Of course not."

She said goodnight rather sadly. When she reached the door she opened it very cautiously a few inches, peering out. Not till she was satisfied that there was no one in sight did she creep out.

8

IT is a pity I am not more time-conscious. I did not look at my watch either when Sonia left me or when I was awakened, but I gather the first was about eleven o'clock and the second between half past twelve and one. Nor do I know exactly what sound disturbed me. The first thing I knew positively was that a bell was being rung, not an electric bell but something like a church bell.

Pulling myself together I remembered that beside the front door was a ship's bell on a wrought-iron bracket. It was, I had always supposed, merely for ornament, because there was an electric bell-push below it which was always used. But someone, for reasons of his own, was ignoring this and tugging away at the bell-cord as though determined to wake the whole household.

I had confused ideas that I might be wanted—something connected with Sonia Reid's extraordinary request. Not a lover of my bed at the best of times, I was determined not to be seen in it now and decided to dress. I dressed quickly and pulled on a fur coat, not because it was a cold night but because it was in the small hours and I wanted its comfort.

As I was going downstairs Steve Lawson appeared, also fully dressed. "What's going on?" he asked.

I ignored this and went down to the lounge where I found Mrs Derosse, her niece Christine and a strange noisy couple dressed in what is known as 'holiday attire'. The man was in his late thirties, going bald, startled into a melodramatic manner, the woman a little younger. They were trying to tell some kind of story to Mrs Derosse but it was at first very confused. The man seemed responsible

73

for the actual narrative, while the woman was content with awed or reproachful interpolations.

"The police ought to be told," the man said. "I wouldn't like to be responsible if they're not. There was nothing we could do . . ."

"We've done all we could," said the woman, "and I don't know what'll happen about the boat."

"The police have been told," said Mrs Derosse. "I phoned them just now, as I told you. They are coming at once."

"I suppose that means giving evidence," said the man. "What kind of a holiday shall we have now? I'd like to know. Sitting in court, and that."

"I told you we shouldn't have gone," said the woman, "only you *would* have it."

"Suppose you just tell us what happened?" suggested Christine. "Perhaps you'd like a drink first. Whisky?"

"I shouldn't say no," said the man fervently.

"I don't mind if I do," the woman responded with even more enthusiasm.

"Well, we decided to take out a rowing-boat. Ten shillings an hour it was and you have to give your name and address when you do it. Moonlight Boating they call it and it's one of the extras at the Merrydown Camp where we're staying. You can have a man with you, only being a bit of an oarsman myself . . ."

"I *told* you," interrupted the woman.

"Anyway, we went, and I must say it was lovely out there. Not a bit cold."

"I was frozen," said his wife.

"And the moon on the water, like . . . like . . ."

"Silver," supplied Christine to assist the tempo.

"We came a bit farther than what we ought to have done, perhaps, right along till we was level with this house. It looked interesting, as you might say, standing on its own like that and I wanted to have a look at it. The wife was all for going back because we've got two young children at the camp being looked after by the people in the next bungalow who are ever so nice and offered."

"We don't really know them," his wife reminded him. "For all we know, Elizabeth and Doreen . . ."

"Haven't I told you not to worry? Well, we were just thinking of turning back when we noticed this one window lit up in the house."

"Which window?" asked Christine.

"The one at the top. Facing out to sea. It was the only window with any light on and it stood out from the rest of the house, as you might say. I'd been wondering if the house was empty it was so dark, when I saw this window lit up like a stage. Well, that's what it looked like."

"It's a pity you hadn't done what I asked you and turned back long ago. Then we shouldn't have all this."

"Still, it was like a stage, wasn't it, Frede? You will admit that. 'It's like a stage,' I said when I saw it, and the wife said, 'Yes, isn't it?'"

"Stage or no stage, it was time we turned back."

"I was looking up at it when I saw someone sitting there. So I pulled in towards the land a bit to take a look from nearer."

"It's a pity you couldn't mind your own business."

"After a while I could see it distinctly. There was a girl sitting on a kind of balcony in front of the window, smoking a cigarette. She seemed to be enjoying the night just as we were."

"*You* were," said his wife.

"I shouldn't have taken any more notice. I said to the wife: 'She's enjoying the night, same as we are,' and that was that, so far as I was concerned. Only I thought we'd gone a bit too close in to the land and decided to pull

75

out to sea. So I was facing the house, as you might say, and the wife had her back to it."

"I never saw anything," said his wife, and there seemed to be a touch of regret in this.

"All of a sudden . . . I wonder if I might trouble you for another drop of Scotch? My nerves are all anywhere, as you can imagine. Whoa! Whoa!" he spoke emphatically but none too soon. "Yes, all of a sudden as I was watching her, this girl . . ."

"It doesn't bear thinking about," said his wife.

"Well, no it doesn't. I can't think what possessed her. She seemed to be quite comfortable there a minute before. Smoking a cigarette, she was. Same as you or me."

"Get on and tell them what happened."

"All of a sudden she seemed to take a dive over the edge. You could see her arms go up. She never made a sound as far as I could hear. And down she went. Must have been right on the rocks below . . ."

Steve Lawson, who had been standing there quite motionless, suddenly cried "Sonia!" and dashed from the room. We heard the front door.

"Is that her husband?" asked the woman in an awed voice.

No one answered.

"Can you get down to the sea from here?" asked the man more intelligently. "I suppose that's where he's gone. He won't find much of her, I'm afraid. Do you think I ought to go with him?"

"You stay where you are," said his wife. "You've done quite enough. It isn't as though she could be alive after that, is it?"

I had a feeling that someone ought to go with Steve Lawson and was glad when Jerrison came in just then.

Christine was very calm. "There's been an accident," she told Jerrison. "Sonia Reid has fallen from the balcony of the tower room. Steve Lawson has gone down. Do you think you could? The police will be here in a few minutes."

Jerrison nodded and left us.

"That path is dangerous at night," said Mrs Derosse.

"They both know it. Jerrison will surely take a torch," Christine told her.

"It's a nasty thing to run into on anyone's holiday," said the man.

"And what'll happen to the boat I don't know," said his wife.

"I just pulled it up on the sand as best I could, but if the tide comes up a bit it'll soon be carried away, I suppose."

"Then you'll have to pay for it. It'll serve you right for not doing as I said and rowing straight back to the camp."

"I couldn't do that. Not with someone *gone* like that. I had to come up and tell you what had happened. I was the only witness, remember."

"You'll get witness when you have to spend the rest of your holidays giving evidence."

"If you pulled the boat up," said Christine, "I wonder you didn't walk along the beach to where she had fallen."

"Couldn't," said the man. "The water was up near the headland."

Christine nodded. "It wasn't deep," she said. "But you couldn't know that. It's just where the rocks jut out."

"He did the best he could," said the woman resentfully, "and very likely lost the boat for his trouble. I should have thought anyone would be satisfied. How we're to get home I don't know. The children will be out of their minds. Well, it's the last time I go moonlight boating, that's one thing."

"Whatever made her do it?" asked the man of Mrs

77

Derosse. "She must have been out of her mind. Diving off like that."

"There's one point," I ventured to say, "which you all seem to be taking rather for granted. I suppose it *was* Sonia Reid?"

This made Mrs Derosse and Christine turn towards me.

"But it was from her room," said Christine.

"I know. Still . . ."

At last the bishop appeared, opportunely I considered. Hasty explanations were made and he at once volunteered to make a round of the house and see who was missing. Christine rose to accompany him.

"The police are a long time," reflected the man. "It's always the way when you want them."

"They have to come from Belstock," Mrs Derosse told them. I must say she seemed very cool for a woman who had just heard of the violent death of one of her guests.

"To think we might have been back at the camp and asleep now," said the woman. "What we shall tell Mr and Mrs Wickers I don't know—leaving them with the children till all hours."

"Tell them the truth," said the man. "They can't blame you when they hear what's happened, can they?"

Did I see a faint smile on the woman's sunburnt and peeling face? Perhaps the thought of the story she would have to tell tomorrow was some compensation to her.

The bishop and Christine came back.

"The door is locked," said Christine. "Sonia's room, I mean. All the rest are in their rooms, except Steve Lawson and Jerrison, of course. I'm afraid most of them will come down now."

"Locked?" repeated Mrs Derosse.

"Yes. I wanted to break it in but the bishop thinks we should wait for the police."

"There!" said the woman. "That shows she meant to

do it, doesn't it? Locking herself in, like that. You'd think people would have more consideration."

This brought no reply.

The rest of that night I shall describe briefly, though it seemed endless at the time and there was daylight before we eventually got to bed.

Two plain-clothes men arrived from Belstock and seemed reasonably efficient. They took statements from everyone, including the man and woman, who were afterwards taken back to their camp in a police-car, the police promising to see what could be done about their boat. It was recovered, I heard afterwards, and returned to its owner.

The door of Sonia's room was opened, but no one except the police was allowed to enter. They spent a considerable time there that night, and early on the following morning others were there for an hour or more, looking for fingerprints I presumed.

Lawson and Jerrison returned and, though Lawson was almost incoherent, Jerrison was able to give the police a description of what they had found. It was not, I was told, for me to hear, though Mrs Jerrison later gave me very horrid descriptions of it.

My informant was again Mrs Jerrison when I heard that, after considerable searching, the original key of Sonia's room was found on the rocks not far from the body, which meant, according to Mrs Jerrison, that it had been in her hand when she fell.

I did not see the couple again before the inquest, when I heard that their name was Grimburn—Lionel and Freda Grimburn, of Grays, Essex. But already on the night of the tragedy I gained a hint of how the story would develop with their growing narrative enthusiasm as time went on. As we heard it first it was fairly simply that of a girl sitting quietly on a balcony then diving—this word was never omitted—into space. The police got a rather more vivid version. "There she was, framed in the lighted window like someone in a picture one minute and in the next she had gone crashing to her death on the rocks below." "How do you know that?" asked one of the policemen, for this was before the return of Lawson and Jerrison. "Well, it stands to reason," said Mr Grimburn. "From that height, I mean."

By the time the coroner heard the story it had further embellishments. She had looked peaceful up there. The Grimburns couldn't help noticing how peaceful she looked. Then—ough, it was like a bird taking off. Only she wasn't a bird, poor thing. She went straight down. Like a stone. To be killed instantly on the rocks. It was horrible. The Grimburns would never get over it. Never. The most horrible thing they'd ever seen.

I wondered, in my no doubt heartless way, how many times they had already told the story in the Merrydown Holiday Camp, and how many more times they would tell it to reporters and to friends when they returned to Grays.

Meanwhile, I myself said nothing about Sonia's visit to me that evening and I was relieved to find that no one, so far as I could judge, had any inkling of it. I suppose it was my duty to give full details of it to the police, but I was able to answer their few questions without lying and salved my conscience that way. I did not want to become any further involved and if this had, as it seemed, been suicide, I did not see what purpose would be served by anyone knowing that she had tried to leave some document with me.

But I wondered what had become of it. Had she hidden it somewhere in the house or persuaded another guest or one of the Derosses to take charge of it?

I tried Mrs Jerrison. "I wonder what became of her

bag," I said. "That would surely help to show whether it was suicide or not. A woman wouldn't jump to her death with her bag in her hand, would she?"

"She didn't," said Mrs Jerrison positively. "I know that because I saw one of the policemen taking it out of the house with him. They must have found it in her room. Though what they found in it I can't say."

Perhaps the strangest part of the whole thing was the silence in which it took place. The Grimburns heard no sound from Sonia and, if she had made any, surely Mrs Derosse in the room below, with an open window, would have heard it. But she says she heard nothing.

9

THESE were the last words in Helena Gort's journal and Carolus put it down and looked at his watch. Twenty past three. He did not hesitate or ponder over what he had read but reached for the switch and, leaving himself in darkness, turned over to sleep.

Helena Gort came down to breakfast, moving as usual without hesitation.

"What do you think about it?" she asked at once.

"I'm going there," said Carolus. "I'm distinctly interested. But I don't think you'd better come with me. Send for your things and go somewhere else."

"What on earth do you mean?"

"You know just what I mean. It's dangerous."

Helena laughed. "Oh don't be absurd. What danger can there be for me?"

"My dear Helena, that is precisely what Sonia Reid

81

thought. You yourself describe her, on the very night of her death, as being apparently quite unafraid."

"Then you think she was murdered?"

Carolus was silent a moment. "Unlike the coroner's," he said at least, "mine would be an open verdict at this point."

"If so, there was some *reason* in her case. What reason could there possibly be in mine?"

"You say 'possibly'. I can tell you a possible reason straight away. I don't say probable, mind you. Suppose there is someone in that house to whom the document Sonia wanted you to take means life or death. Suppose that he or she—shall we say?—caused Sonia's death in order to obtain possession of it. Suppose in the meantime she had handed it to someone else or hidden it, so that the murderer failed to obtain it. Suppose the murderer knew she went to see you that evening. None of those suppositions are far-fetched and they do point inevitably to danger for you."

"I'm certainly going back," said Helena Gort. "For one thing, I doubt if you would get in without me. You're my nephew or my stepson or something. Mrs Derosse has her niece to 'put things right', surely I can have a nephew to look after me?"

"I see your point. I still think you should move."

"No one will know who you are," went on Helena Gort as though she had not heard him. "It isn't as though you were one of these really famous investigators. You just come to stay and use your eyes and ears. I'm going back anyway, so if you really think there's danger in the place you ought to come."

"I will."

When Carolus told Mrs Stick that he would like her to have a good holiday and therefore intended to close the house, her feelings seemed to be mixed.

"I'm not saying we shouldn't like a bit of a holiday," she said. "Especially if we can get down to Clacton. Stick dearly loves a day's shrimping and there's nothing does his sciatica good like the salt water. Only how are we to enjoy ourselves when we daren't so much as pick the paper up in the morning for fear of seeing you mixed up in something? I was only saying to Stick, we shan't be able to see a paper next, not without not knowing whether you haven't got yourself into trouble. I did think this lady, a friend of your mother's and that, would know better than to lead you into anything, but no, there it was, 'suspects'. I heard it as plain as could be. What *are* we to think?"

"You go and have your holiday," said Carolus. "You won't see my name in any papers, I promise you."

"I'm sure I hope not, sir."

At eleven o'clock Carolus and Helena drove off in his Bentley Continental, the car which one of his colleagues on the school staff had called 'a piece of sheer exhibitionism'.

"You know," said Carolus, "I don't think your idea of my being your nephew is a very good one. I think I'd rather chance Mrs Derosse not admitting me, but say straight out that you have invited me because I've got a certain amount of experience of this sort of thing. After all, unless she has anything to conceal she ought to be glad rather than sorry."

"And her guests?"

"It's not as though I am a policeman. They'll probably want to talk—most of them."

"Just as you think, Carolus. I have a feeling that Christine won't be too pleased."

"Oh. Why?"

"I don't know. She has a reputation for being able to handle things herself."

"We can only try."

They were successful but perhaps only because Christine was out when they reached Cat's Cradle and they interviewed Mrs Derosse alone.

"There *is* a room, isn't there?" said Helena at once. "The one Christine had before she moved into the room in the tower."

"Yes, there is a room. I wasn't thinking of letting it while things are like this."

Carolus longed to ask 'like what?' but resisted it.

"Mr Deene is a very old friend of mine, Mrs Derosse. In fact I knew his mother. He has a flair for clearing up mysteries of this sort and I've no doubt would soon have your place back to its old self."

"You mean, he's a detective?"

Carolus wished his least favourite pupil Rupert Priggley could hear this. It would make him wince.

"Nothing so old-fashioned," said Helena. "He just seems to sense how these things happen."

"I don't think Christine would be very pleased. She wants to clear this up herself."

"Oh come now, Mrs Derosse. I'm simply asking you to let a room to my old friend Carolus Deene."

"I don't see how I can refuse. But I do hope it's not going to cause more trouble."

"You do want the whole thing dissipated, don't you?"

Mrs Derosse tried a feeble retort. "But it is. Sonia's death has been proved suicide and Lydia Mallister's we know was her heart."

"Then why, if there is nothing strange about all this, are your guests in a state which I can only call one of terror? Why does everyone lock his door and watch every move of the others? Why have they all got the jitters?"

Mrs Derosse sat down rather heavily.

"I know," she said.

Helena followed her advantage.

"Do you think Lydia Mallister died naturally? Do you believe Sonia committed suicide?"

"No," admitted Mrs Derosse. "Yet I don't see how either of them could be murder."

"Carolus will," said Helena confidently, forgetting the object of the argument. "He's capable of finding a murder in any set of circumstances, I assure you."

"But I don't want . . ."

"It would clear the air," said Helena finally and the arrangement was made.

But, as Mrs Derosse and Helena anticipated, it did not please Christine. She drove up half an hour later in her pale-blue sports car and gave a disdainful look at the Bentley as she passed it. She must have heard from her aunt the identity of its owner because, when she came into the lounge to find Helena and Carolus alone, she was obviously controlling great annoyance.

"Oh, Christine," said Helena pleasantly, "this is Carolus Deene."

"I know," said Christine with a short nod, "my aunt told me you had come to stay here. I'm sorry I was out. I will tell you frankly, Mr Deene, I should have asked her not to let you have a room."

Carolus smiled. "I'm an undesirable?"

"In the circumstances, yes. I know all about you. I've read your cases. I can quite see that this must be a nice little mystery for you. Just the sort of thing you like. But does it ever occur to you, Mr Deene, that people's lives are not all crossword puzzles for your amusement? My aunt has her living to make. It's rather more important to us than providing you with an intriguing summer holiday."

"I'm sorry you should feel that. I do enjoy trying to find the truth in complicated cases. I won't deny it. But I don't think of people as chess pieces, either, Miss Derosse.

If your aunt is the innocent victim of circumstances, I shall do all I can to be of assistance to her."

Christine swung round, flushed with anger. "*If* my aunt," she said, "*If* my aunt is innocent! Are you suggesting . . ."

"Miss Derosse, you must surely know that I must approach this with an open mind. It naturally seems absurd to you who know your aunt and are fond of her . . ."

Suddenly Christine smiled. "I was forgetting that part of the formula," she said.

"Thank you," said Carolus.

"I'll admit this, so far as I know anything about you, you don't look for publicity. What I dislike is that this place which is my aunt's pride, in fact her whole life, should be turned into a sort of haunted house at the fair."

"That," said Carolus, "has happened already, with two deaths, police inquiries, and an inquest. I'm not raising the dust any further. There can't really be much peace here till you know the truth, even if the truth is just what it appears to be to the outsider."

"I want to know the truth, too," said Christine.

"Then help me to find it."

Christine considered. "I won't obstruct you," she said.

"You won't tell me all you know?"

"All I know? What do you think I know about it that the police don't?"

"Quite a lot. For instance, what did Sonia Reid talk to you about on the night of her death?"

"To me?"

"Yes, Miss Derosse."

"I don't remember her talking to me that night."

"You don't? She did not ask you a favour, by any chance?"

86

Christine pulled at her cigarette.

"So you've started already. And on me. What makes you think Sonia would ask me a favour?"

"Because you were probably the only person in the house she could trust."

"What favour?"

"Just to look after something."

"I don't know what you're talking about."

"All right, Miss Derosse. Only I thought you were not going to obstruct me."

"I didn't promise to help you, either. Let's have a drink," said Christine. She seemed to feel some relief.

"Where are you going to start?" she asked Carolus over a dry martini.

"In the holiday camp, of course."

"Have you ever been to one?"

"No."

"You'll find it fascinating. What do you think Mr and Mrs Grimburn can tell you?"

"Too much, I'm afraid. I should think their story by now is so over-rehearsed that it will be difficult to extract any of its pristine truth. But I can try."

"You can. You certainly won't have any difficulty in making them talk."

"You see, that does seem to be the crux of the thing. What caused that young woman to go hurtling off into space? Was it pre-determined or accidental? Voluntary or involuntary? These are the first questions, aren't they? It's the old trio—murder, suicide or accident. It just might be that something those moonlight boaters saw will help me judge that."

"I shouldn't be too hopeful. And you'll have to hear a lot more."

Carolus grinned. "I'm rather used to that. It's nearly always too much—or too little."

Bishop Grissell came in and Christine introduced Carolus, explaining his identity.

"Not much in my line, I'm afraid," said the bishop, stoutly.

When his sister joined them she was even more direct. "You mean you're a detective?" she snorted at Carolus.

"I'm a schoolmaster," replied Carolus smugly. "But with insatiable curiosity."

Phiz said: "Phuh!"

"He asks the most devastating questions," said Christine, beginning to enjoy herself. "He'll probably ask you where you were on the night of the crime, Miss Grissell."

"What crime?" asked Phiz loftily.

"The first," said Carolus. "The death of Lydia Mallister." He watched her closely.

"Have I walked into a mad-house?" asked Phiz.

Carolus resisted the temptation to say 'Not yet'. "Don't worry, Miss Grissell," he said. "I shan't ask any questions you don't want to answer."

"That's impudent," said Phiz.

"I'm sorry. I meant it to be reassuring."

"Have you any official status in this matter?"

"Oh, none whatever."

"Then why should we be expected to answer any questions of yours?"

"People sometimes want to help me arrive at the truth."

"Jesting Pilate, eh?" said the bishop heartily. "Phiz, my dear, I've no doubt Mr Deene means to be helpful."

When the Gee-Gees appeared they were even more conciliatory than the bishop. Miss Grey, it appeared, had read books about Carolus's investigations and was most interested, she said, to meet him.

"Particularly if you manage to relieve us all of our

doubts over this nasty series of incidents, Mr Deene. This was, I assure you, a most peaceful and happy little community before . . ."

"Yes, Miss Grey; before what?" asked Carolus.

Miss Grey was confused.

"Well, I suppose . . ."

Miss Godwin came to her assistance.

"Before Lydia Mallister's death," she said firmly.

The Natterleys did not appear before lunch, but when the meal was over they waited for Carolus to be introduced to them.

"We understand that you are here to investigate," said the Major. "We would like you to know that anything we can tell you that may assist you is entirely at your disposal."

"We have tried not to involve ourselves in the talk which has followed these very unpleasant events," his wife added. "But naturally, living in the house, it has been impossible for us not to observe and hear certain things."

"You will find we have a certain amount of information which will be of the greatest importance to you," stated Major Natterley. "And when you reach a point in your investigations at which it will be helpful to you we shall be only too ready to give it to you."

Carolus sighed. He knew that readiness.

"It's very kind of you," he said.

"We make it a principle not to concern ourselves with other people's affairs. We lead very much our own life here, as you will observe. But in my years in the army . . ."

"What branch?" asked Carolus.

"Actually, the Pay Corps. In my years in the army I formed certain habits of observation which have stood me in good stead. We both, in fact, while never wishing to be inquisitive, cannot help but see and hear. We are only too anxious that all our doubts shall be relieved."

"Was Sonia Reid a friend of yours?"

The question seemed to shock, if not horrify, the Natterleys. The Major was the first to regain his composure sufficiently to speak.

"We cannot make it too plain," he said, "that we have never had anything approaching friendship with anyone in this house. We believe in civility, but there we wish it to end. Such friends as we have, and they are few, are in no way associated with Cat's Cradle—people of a very different stamp. We are not, we hope, snobbish but anything more than the merest acquaintanceship would be quite impossible for us with other members of this household. The unfortunate girl you mention may on occasion have been one of a conversational circle of which we have briefly, quite briefly, formed a part. Nothing more."

"Pity. I'd like to know something about her."

"It is not impossible," said Major Natterley, "that we can, from remote observation, give you some information on that score. But do not ask us, pray, for intimate knowledge of her character or antecedents."

"I won't. What about Lydia Mallister?"

"There again, our habit of retiring to our own sitting-room . . ."

"Quite. Well, I hope we can have a talk some time. I appreciate your co-operation."

Before the evening was over Carolus had met the entire household, except the staff. He was warned that he would find Steve Lawson a man very much changed since his appearance in Helena's diary as a fleshy and properous youngish race-horse-owner. He found, in fact, a surly fellow whose clothes looked as though he had lost weight. He was not exactly uncivil to Carolus, but he made it clear that he should not seek his acquaintance. Carolus did his innocent blunderer act.

"I gather you were very friendly with Sonia Reid?" he said blandly.

"Sorry, Mr Deene. I don't talk about Sonia."

This was curt and to the point and left even Carolus at a loss for a moment.

"I expect you've had quite enough of it with police inquiries. I'm sorry if I . . ."

"That's all right. You've got a job to do, I suppose. But I don't talk. I hope you understand that. Not in the witness box, not when the police ask questions, and not chattily with you, or anyone else."

"You make it very clear. I only hope you will be able to keep to your resolve."

"What do you mean?"

"I could imagine circumstances in which it would be difficult. But not with me, Mr Lawson. You won't be badgered by me."

Lawson looked surly and puzzled, but said nothing.

Carolus met James Mallister and Esmée Welton together, as they were usually found nowadays. He had the impression, which they had also given to Helena, that they were quite hopelessly and sincerely in love.

"I wish you would get rid of this wretched business," said Mallister in his rather sad voice. "It's been appalling for us, you know."

The 'us' was a quieter and less aggressive thing than the repetitive 'us' of the Natterleys.

"You've probably been told already," said Esmée, "that James and I want to get married."

"Indeed I have. By more than one person," smiled Carolus.

"You probably wonder why we don't. But, you see, neither of us has any relatives or roots anywhere else to speak of and to get married from this house as it is at present would be rather ill-omened, wouldn't it? "

" I suppose so."

" You've probably been told all the rest," said Esmée—"how heartless we were to think of one another when Lydia was dying, and all that. The truth is, James was a saint with Lydia, Mr Deene. She had a wicked tongue and you don't know what he had to put up with."

" At all events," said Mallister, " do try to find out what it is that has made us all feel and behave like this since her death."

" I'm really as much concerned with Sonia Reid's death. Do you think there was any connection? "

They seemed to think about this and answered reasonably.

" I don't see how there can have been," said Mallister. " But it came while everyone was still talking about Lydia and . . ."

" The whole thing is beastly," said Esmée. " I don't suppose it will be any less so when we know the truth, but at least then we shall know where we are, as we used to say. I for one am glad you've come."

" Thanks for that. I get rather tired of being looked on as a sort of vulture, swooping down on dead bodies."

Esmée smiled. " You don't look much like a vulture," she said. " If there is to be any talk of vultures, I should have thought ' Phiz my dear' qualifies splendidly."

" Now, Esmée, don't be bitchy," said Mallister.

" You've only got to look at her," said Esmée. " I don't know what kind of a noise vultures make, but it can't be very different from that voice and the things she says. However, I'll do as James says and try not to be bitchy."

10

So the first impression Carolus had of Cat's Cradle was not like Helena's. He saw, that day, very little sign of tension and none of fear. Either these had passed with the death of Sonia Reid and the inquest which followed it, or everyone was putting up a show of confidence and indifference for his benefit. But he had not been long in the house before he understood what Helena had meant.

During the morning he persuaded Christine to let him make a thorough examination of the house, noting who occupied which rooms. She took him first to her own, 'the room in the tower', and he spent some time there.

"What on earth is this huge table for?" he asked, for the centre of the room was occupied by a square deal table over which was an old-fashioned table-cloth.

"Sonia asked for it," said Christine. "She used to bring work home from the business and had a typewriter here. I haven't got rid of it because I'm not staying long."

He went out to the little balcony and sat on its stone balustrade as Sonia must have done. "She must have felt very confident," he remarked.

"She often sat there, apparently," said Christine. "As you see there's not room for a chair out here, and the view's rather fine, isn't it?"

"Yes. If you don't look down."

Christine smiled. "I thought you were a paratrooper," she said.

"I was, but I don't like heights."

The only other room which occupied him long was the Mallisters' and here he opened the door of a built-in cupboard.

"Yes, it's a solidly built house," said Christine. "The walls can take these. They're too narrow for clothes, though."

"Have all the rooms got them?" asked Carolus.

"Most of them. There's one in the next room to this, which must be about here." She tapped the wall near the cupboard doors.

"Let's see, who lives there?"

"The Gee-Gees."

They completed their round of the house and walked down the cliff path to where the body was found. Carolus made no relevant comment.

In the afternoon he drove over to the Merrydown Holiday Camp. At five o'clock he reached the imposing entrance, built in concrete to represent the gateway of a mediaeval castle, complete with imitation watch-towers and imitation drawbridge. He drove in without impediment, however, and, parking his car, went to the central reception desk. A smooth gentleman looked up from his papers.

"Can you help me?" asked Carolus. "I want to find some people named Grimburn."

The receptionist's reaction was violent. "God!" he said. "Not another! I thought every blasted newspaper in the country had done them. What are you. *The Methodist Recorder* or the *Catholic Herald*? Or *Sports and Hobbies*? They're the only ones left."

"I'm not a newspaperman," said Carolus mildly.

"Police, then?"

"No."

"Don't start telling me you're just an old friend of theirs? We've had that one till we're sick of it."

"No. I've never met them. I'm staying at Cat's Cradle. I just want a chat with them."

The receptionist eyed him cunningly. "Advertising?"

he suggested. "They saw the whole thing through Somebody's field glasses or something?"

Carolus shook his head and waited patiently.

"I tell you what," the receptionist said. "They can't be called over the loud-speakers again. There's strict orders from the Top about that. The other campers are sick of it. Grimburns wanted all day long. If you can find them you're welcome. I can't do any more."

"Could you tell me the number of their room . . . hut . . . tent . . ."

"Their *chalet* is number 1017. In the East Block. But they won't be in it now."

"Where will they be?"

"How on earth am I to know? They may be taking part in the All-Europe Athletic Sports in the Chattaway Stadium. They could be watching the Inter-Block Cricket Match. There's a lecture by Bubbles Flynn in the Montgomery Lecture Hall. The Swimming Gala is going on in the Woodland Pool, and the Junior Competition in the Bluewater Baths. Of course, as Grimburn apparently knows how to row, they may be in the Grand Trafalgar Regatta. If they were older people, I'd say they were in one of the cinemas or at the concert in the Jazz-Philharmonica Hall or watching the Snooker Championship."

"Mightn't they be in their own quarters?"

"Not likely. No television in the chalets, you see. Only in the Olde Television Inne. We found it ruinous to the bar trade. You can try, of course. It's only about half a mile's walk from here. Then they might have gone on the Mountain Ramble. Or the Mass Picnic. Or the Anti-Nuclear Jamboree. There's the Ice Rink, too, but the show's not on till tomorrow—*Strip Glacé.* Do they play tennis, do you know? The Inter-House Finals are on today."

"There seems to be quite a choice," said Carolus.

"You might try the Bingo Palace. Or the Repertory Theatre."

"Couldn't I catch them at a meal-time?"

"Very difficult, old man. We've got eight dining-halls, you know."

"Eight?"

"Yes. All different. There's the Parisian, the London Particular, the Neapolitan, the Yorkshire . . ."

"You mean to say . . ."

"Hold it, old man. The Delicatessen, the Samovar, the Valenciana and the Viennese."

"You mean you have eight kinds of catering?"

"Well, between you and me, there's only one kitchen. It's the decorations of the rooms that vary, and the wording of the menu. It wouldn't do to have them all the same. People would call that regimentation, and that's what they complain about with holiday camps. Must give them variety."

"I see."

"It's all right till it comes to finding anyone. Then you don't know where you are, because there are three shifts with each restaurant. Take these Grimburns you want to find. How's anyone to know which they fancy? You don't happen to know if they've got a yen for anything Viennese, do you? Or good old English? Or Frenchified? We might have a try if you knew that."

"I'm afraid I don't."

"There you are. They're probably like all the rest of them, popping from one to another. Italian one day, Spanish the next."

"But you say the food's the same?"

"It's the names that vary, old man. There's a lot in a name, you know. Call something *côtelette à la Milanaise* and nobody's going to think it's a mutton cutlet, except those in the London Particular restaurant who say they do like this good old English fare. See what I mean? You need a bit of psychology."

"You seem to have it. You should go far," said Carolus admiringly.

"Well, I've got some ideas of my own. Nobody's thought of introducing Speed Trials here, yet. Still, you want to find the Grimburns. I shouldn't waste time on the dining-halls if I was you."

"What about in a bar this evening?"

"That's possible. But if you don't know what they look like, it won't be easy. There are six Olde Innes, you see. There's the Falstaff Olde Inne, the Sputnik Olde Inne, the . . ."

"Yes, yes. I see the idea."

"Sorry I can't be more helpful. Only, as I say, we've got strict orders not to use the buzzer. Best hope is through inquiries. They've become pretty well known through all this publicity. Try asking our Campers' Pals. They're the ones wearing orange-coloured trousers and green shirts. They may be able to help you."

"Thanks," said Carolus and went off to try his luck. Coming to a long row of shops he decided to try an inquiry at the Antique and Souvenir Arcade and found a helpful young woman.

"Yes, I know them," she said. "Had their pictures in the paper last week, didn't they? They were in here only this morning buying some postcards and a miniature souvenir warming-pan. I *think* they said they were going to the Wigan Pier Pierrot Show this afternoon. That's in the Palm Pavilion, about twenty minutes' walk towards the sea."

"Thanks. I'll try their . . . chalet first. It's in the East Block, I understand."

"Yes. You go down here, past the Indian Fortune-

Teller's Kiosk and the Elizabethan Ice Cream Parlour. Then turn right by the New Eiffel Tower and there you are. All those rows of chalets are the East Block. You've got the number?"

Carolus followed these instructions and found himself in a vast chessboard of identical bathing-huts painted orange and green. After a quarter of an hour of hard walking he stood triumphantly before Number 1017. Its door was closed but he decided to knock. The only response was the opening of the door of 1019, beside it. A thin woman, whose skin had turned a fiery red in the sun, looked at him disapprovingly. "They're not in," she said.

"No. I wonder whether you could help me . . ."

"No, I couldn't. We've had quite enough of the newspapers and that coming to take pictures of them just because they happened to be out there at the time."

"I suppose it made them news," said Carolus bravely.

"News? I should think it did. There's Her in the *Daily Mirror*, grinning on both sides of her face as though it was something to be proud of, and Him in the *Daily Express* with an oar in his hand, as though he was in the Oxford and Cambridge. It's enough to make you sick. Who was looking after the children all the time, that's what I should like to know. And little Doreen not telling me she wanted to Go Somewhere so that I had it to clear up."

"Are you Mrs Wickers?" asked Carolus gratefully, remembering the name from Helena's journal.

"That's right. However did you know? No one's been to ask me anything about that evening, though we never got a wink of sleep till they came home full of it about a girl jumping out of a window. I don't see much in that. When there was a fire three doors from me, they was all jumping out of the windows like grasshoppers."

"Perhaps there isn't much to it," agreed Carolus. "That's really what I want to know. I think it has all been rather exaggerated. I've been sent to investigate."

"You mean, you think it may all be a lot of talk, and them walking about as though they'd been to the North Pole?"

"Undoubtedly a girl died that night after falling from a window, but whether . . ."

"*She* says it was like a film. She says they saw it all as clear as a picture. I don't see how they could have done from that way away. So you want to see how much they've been exaggerating, do you?"

"That's about it. Do you know where I could find them?"

"Not now, I don't. They may have gone to listen to the Connaught Rangers Band down on the Camp Promenade, or perhaps they're in the Treasure Hunt. But I tell you what. My husband and I always go with them to one of the bars about eight o'clock as soon as they've put the children to bed. They're all right when they're not on about this girl jumping out of a window. Quite nice people till their heads got turned by all those reporters. We've been about together quite a bit. So when we go up for a drink tonight I could look out for you and introduce you. Then perhaps you can make them see it's not the end of the world when someone has a bit of an accident and they happen to catch a glimpse of it."

"Thanks. But which bar will you be in?"

"Oh, that's the trouble. We like to get round a bit. We don't usually stay in one place. They're all done out different, you see. There's the Rock an' Roll Olde Inne, where Bugs Wriggly and his Band play. And the Space Travel Olde Inne, where it's all got up with rockets and that, and the barmen wear space suits. Or we might be in the Beatnik Olde Inne—that's proper old-fashioned but a bit quiet because the older people seem to go there. You can't tell, really. But I'll be looking out for you."

"It's very kind of you."

"Well, I hope you take them down a peg, that's all."

"Thank you, Mrs Wickers. I'll try to find you this evening."

"I'd ask you to wait for them, only there's nowhere to sit, really. Just the two beds in our chalet and they're all untidy at the moment. Besides they'll only just pop in and put Doreen and Elizabeth to bed and out they'll go again."

Carolus started on his walk back towards the entrance round which the Olde Innes were clustered. It was past six now and he entered the Major Gagarin Olde Inne for a much-needed whisky-and-soda. He found it a barn-like place in which a bar ran down the entire length of the room—some sixty feet long. The walls were stencilled with suitable designs and the barmen wore what he could only suppose was the uniform of Russian space-travellers off duty, a curious mixture of the Martian and the Cossack.

"Oughtn't to serve you, really," said the barman in very un-Russian tones.

"How's that?"

"You're not wearing your camper's badge. It wouldn't be so bad if you had your house-tie on, or your Old Merrydownian blazer. How am I to know you're a camper?"

"Don't I look like one?"

"S'hard to say. We get all sorts. Still, I'll serve you this time. Whisky? Most of them have vodka in here."

"I'll stick to whisky."

"This was the Spanish Toreador Olde Inne last year," confided the barman. "Then it was all sherry we served.

Only they believe in keeping bang up to date, so we've turned over to this get-up and vodka. Between you and me, I'd rather we were back to the Gay Paree Inne which we were two years ago."

"The whirligig of time," reflected Carolus.

"That's it. I don't know what they'll think of for next year. I suppose it depends what happens in the world."

By nine o'clock Carolus had visited all the Olde Innes and found them identical in shape and size, varying only in their murals and the costumes of the attendants. He liked best the Beatnik Olde Inne, which was served by ladies whose lank hair and curious costume could not hide the fact that they were nice healthy girls from the northern counties. But he saw nothing of Mrs Wickers.

He decided to start the round again and found his barman at the Major Gagarin pulling beer taps. "I knew they'd come back to wallop," he told Carolus.

Just then Carolus saw at a table in a far corner the fiery face of Mrs Wickers. She was signalling enthusiastically and he saw that she was with two men and another woman. He went across and found himself at last facing Mr and Mrs Grimburn. But they were not at once as communicative as they might have been. Mr Grimburn, in fact, was cagey. "I hear you want me to tell you The Story," he said.

"If you wouldn't mind," said Carolus, calling a Cossack Astronaut to order a round of drinks.

"Bit late for it, aren't you? We've had all the papers to see us."

Carolus explained that he was concerned only in trying to find out the truth about Sonia Reid's death and added that, of course, Mr and Mrs Grimburn were the only people who could tell him that.

"Of course we are," put in Mrs Grimburn. "No one else was watching her, were they?"

"Not so far as is known," said Carolus.

The Grimburns exchanged apprehensive glances. "Think there may have been?" asked the man.

"People don't always like coming forward in a case like this," Carolus told him. "Anyway, so far as we know, you are the only ones whose information is valuable." This was perhaps unfortunately phrased.

"It doesn't seem to have been of much value yet," said Mr Grimburn. "Not to pay for our holiday, really. There was one or two cheques, but you'd have thought one of the Sunday papers would have wanted a life-story. With all that publicity."

"I don't know much about newspapers. I'm really trying to get this cleared up for the sake of those in the house. It has been very uncomfortable for them. There's still a sort of mystery about it."

"I should think there was. That's what I told one of the newspapers. One of the greatest mysteries of modern times, I said. I mean, *why* did she do it?"

"You think she did 'do it'? Deliberately, I mean?"

"Ah, now you're asking. I don't see why I shouldn't tell you the whole story."

Carolus resigned himself.

"It was getting on for eleven o'clock when we went down to the Camp Promenade for a bit of a stroll. The band had finished playing and there weren't many about. It was a lovely night, though, with a bit of a moon and we came down to this notice which said *Moonlight Boating 10/- an hour. 21/- with a Jolly Jack sailor.* So I said to the wife, 'What say we have a bit of a row?'"

Carolus nodded, determined to show no impatience.

"She was all for it at first. She knew I'm an oarsman and the sea was smooth as glass. But when we'd got out towards that headland she wanted to go back. She'd got the two little girls to think of, which Mr and Mrs Wickers here had kindly said they'd look after."

Smiles were exchanged in recognition of this tribute.

"But I said: 'After all, we may as well get our money's worth.' It was about then we noticed this house standing alone on the side of the cliff. 'Looks as though it's haunted,' I said to the wife. 'All up there on its own without a light showing.' She thought it was funny, too. It wasn't until we'd got a bit farther round the headland that we saw, right up at the top of the house, this one lighted window."

Mrs Grimburn did not interrupt. It was clear that, in her view as in that of her husband, the story had reached perfection and needed no more tampering with.

"I said: 'Let's pull in a bit farther and have a look.' It was then we saw this girl sitting sideways on the little balcony outside her window. You could see her dark shape against the lighted window behind. When we got nearer, we saw she was smoking a cigarette."

"You were near enough to see that it was a girl?"

"Certainly. I couldn't see her face, but from the whole way she was sitting you could tell it wasn't an old woman. We decided to turn back and I was pulling out to sea when it happened."

"So Mrs Grimburn had her back to the lighted window?"

"Just for a minute I had," admitted Mrs Grimburn. "I'd been watching her till then as plain as could be."

"All of a sudden she seemed to put up her arms as though she was going to dive . . ."

"Could you possibly show me how you mean?"

Mr Grimburn obliged. "I don't mean she actually poised for a dive. She didn't seem to stand up, for one thing. She didn't put her palms together like divers do. But her hands went right up in the air and there she was dropping through space."

"You couldn't watch her fall, of course."

"No. Only her take-off, as you might say, while she was in the light of the window."

"You heard nothing?"

"Not a sound. It all seemed to happen too quickly. It was done in an instant. Quite still one moment and over the edge in the next."

"Thank you very much, Mr Grimburn," said Carolus rising. "I'm most grateful to you."

"Don't you want to hear the rest of it—about our going up to the house and that?"

"You've given me the very information I needed," said Carolus truthfully, as he backed away under the disappointed stare of Mrs Wickers. "Thank you very much. Good night to you. Good night Mrs Grimburn, Mrs Wickers."

He had put two yards between himself and the table. But his friend the barman called him as he was making for the door.

"*You're* no camper," he said good-humouredly. "You've come to get a story from those Grimburns, haven't you? I knew as soon as you came in. Did you get what you wanted?"

"Yes," said Carolus. "I did. Rather more than I wanted." He slipped a pound note into the barman's hand.

"It's just on time," said the barman. "You ought to wait and see how they get 'em out. See, we don't shout Time or anything. Wouldn't do. No regimentation, they say."

"No regimentation?" gasped Carolus.

"No. Strictly forbidden."

"But you must have a closing time."

"You wait and see. Here they come!"

Into the bar came a macabre procession led by a small brass band. Behind this were the Campers' Pals in their orange and green uniform, each stooping down and holding the waist of the one in front.

"Come and join us!" played the band. "Come and join us!" sang the Campers' Pals. "Come and join our happy throng!"

They crocodiled round the Olde Inne and, as they did so, every camper in the place swallowed his drink, clutched the waist of the one in front and, singing heartily, moved on. Carolus caught a glimpse of the red and grinning features of Mrs Wickers in the line. In a moment the band was moving on to the next Olde Inne and the room was empty.

"See what I mean?" said the barman. "No regimentation."

11

NEXT morning, at breakfast, Carolus had his first experience of what Helena had described as the 'jitters' of his fellow-guests. He was alone for a time with Bishop Grissell.

The bishop leant across the table and lowered his already deep voice. "Did you hear anything in the night?" he asked.

"No. Slept like a top," said Carolus.

"You didn't hear someone shouting?"

"No. What time was this?"

"In the small hours," said the bishop. "I heard it distinctly. A man's voice."

"Where was he?"

"It was hard to tell. Below us, somewhere. On the beach or in a boat."

"What was he shouting about?"

"I couldn't catch what he said. But I heard the word 'murder' or 'murderer'."

"Some drunk from the holiday camp, probably," suggested Carolus.

The bishop looked at him fixedly. The matter seemed to be a serious one for him. "You may be right. But it wasn't the impression I received at all. It sounded like someone in distress. Perhaps in anger, too."

It had not, however, deprived the bishop of his appetite and Carolus watched a generous English breakfast disappearing.

When Helena appeared later he told her what the bishop had said, but she was not helpful, as she had taken a good dose of sleeping-tablets and would have heard nothing, anyway.

"But it gives me an idea," said Carolus. "What do we know about these people, Helena? Even the bishop. We know he is or was a bishop—Crockford tells us that. But why has he returned at this very early age to live in a guest house? Who *was* Sonia Reid? Where did she come from? And Esmée Welton? The Natterleys are fairly obvious and the Gee-Gees, but the Mallisters seem to have been a rather odd couple. You've told me about Mrs Derosse and her niece, but where did she find the Jerrisons? Why is such an apparently perfect couple, who could make a fortune and retire in ten years in the States, content to stay in this place? Above all, who is Steve Lawson, exactly? You see what I mean. They exist for us only as guests here."

"You think that's important?"

"In some cases, yes. Particularly Sonia Reid. Hadn't she any parents?"

"She had someone described as a foster-mother. Sonia was apparently an orphan, brought up by a Mrs Tukes, who appeared at the funeral. She came from London. I've no doubt Mrs Derosse can give you the address and enough information to start your inquiries on the others if you think they are necessary."

"I do."

"Personally I should have thought you would do better to see the police. They probably know a great deal more than you think."

"Not yet. The police have a job to do and very little use for people like me, naturally enough. My experience is that they will sometimes relax a little and let fall a fact or two, but only if I've got something useful to offer them. I haven't yet."

So Carolus drove away with a number of names and addresses in his pocket, supplied by Mrs Derosse. He would reach London in time for a late lunch at his club, then go to 17 Northumberland Terrace, Forest Hill, in the afternoon. He had hopes of hearing from Sonia Reid's foster-mother something which might help him to account for her behaviour at Cat's Cradle, even if it threw no light on her death. But perhaps more interesting would be his interview, if he obtained it, with Mrs Cremoine Rose of Alexandra Gate, the sister of the late Mrs Mallister. A Mr Arthur Picknet, a solicitor with offices in Bloomsbury, had been given as a reference by Mallister when he first came to Cat's Cradle, and a Reverend Ralph Cracknell was known to be a friend of the bishop's. His only line on Steve Lawson was that he was a member of a small out-of-hours drinking club called the Academics, but he knew that the Jerrisons had been employed at Conway Towers

Preparatory School, Orbiton. It was a nice little directory he carried, he thought, and if he got through this lot in a couple of days he would be lucky. Meanwhile, in view of what he had seen and heard at Cat's Cradle and Merrydown, he was not unduly anxious about Helena for the moment, or indeed about anyone else there.

Mrs Tukes was a sour, heavy party who found movement and speech an effort which made her gasp. She came to the door of her semi-detached grey Victorian house and eyed Carolus with weary caution.

"Oh, it's about Sonia, is it?" she said without animation. "Well, you better come in here because I can't stand talking here. My feet are killing me today."

Carolus found himself in a sitting-room hung with heavy curtains, which looked as if a shake would send out not only clouds of dust but possibly a flight of moths or even bats. He sat on the broken spring of a rexine-covered settee while Mrs Tukes lowered herself noisily into an armchair.

"That's better," she said. "I've been on my feet all day. I feel as though I was done for. I'm on my own, you see, except in the mornings when I have a woman come in for a minute. It's too much for me, really. I ought to be looked after. Now, what is it you want to know about Sonia, because I mustn't talk too much. It tires me out."

"You brought her up, I understand?"

"Yes, the ungrateful little bitch! Excuse my language, but there's no other word really. I slaved away body and soul for that girl and wore my fingers to the bone looking after her."

Carolus, who had a literal mind, could not keep his glance from the pudgy fingers on Mrs Tukes's lap.

"You adopted her?"

"I took her in from the orphans, but what they give

you wouldn't cover the cost of her washing. Night and day I was working to bring her up decent, with never a minute to myself. It wasn't as though she was one to help. It was work, work, work for me, year in and year out, all the time she was there. Then as soon as she started to earn money what happened? "

"What did happen? "

"She was off. Never saw her again, except now and again for decency's sake, when she'd come down here and expect to be waited on hand and foot. I told her. I said: 'Sonia, you expect too much.' But she'd just give that smile of hers and leave me to do the washing up, with my varicose veins nearly killing me."

"How long ago did she leave you? "

"Ten years almost to a week. I remember it as though it was yesterday. I was sitting here where I am now, exhausted with all I'd had to do for her, so tired I could scarcely speak. 'I'm leaving,' she came out with, giving a toss of her head. 'I've had enough of this.' 'Oh, you have?' I said, trying to get my breath. 'After all I've done for you all these years.' 'You've been paid for it,' she says. 'Paid for it? If they'd paid me a hundred pounds a week it wouldn't have covered me for the trouble you've been! ' I was going to say more but she was off out of the house. She'd been cunning enough to pack her bags while I was having five minutes' nap that afternoon. I saw her getting into a car with a man, who I heard afterwards she was living with. No, not that one down where she died. There've been several since this. If the truth were known, she's been little better than a street woman one way and another. Though I believe she always kept her job."

"She was musical? "

"If that's what you call it. There was a piano here when she was a girl, but I had to get rid of it. Thump, thump, thump, till I thought my head would split right open. Instead of helping me in the house as you'd have thought she'd have done, she'd leave me slaving on my knees to get the place a bit clean, while she went on playing away like a barrel-organ. Just when I had one of my head-aches and needed to lie down quiet, she'd begin and nothing would stop her. She'd have gone on half the night if the neighbours on both sides hadn't complained. So when she went off to work it was in a music shop, and I understand she was in one to the last."

"Yes, she was in partnership with a man named Rhodes. Reid and Rhodes, the shop was called. I haven't met Mr Rhodes, but I gather it was a strictly business relationship."

"If it was, it was the first, then," said Mrs Tukes venomously. "She's been kept, to my knowledge, three times. The last time I saw her . . ."

"When was that?"

"Only a month or two back. She drove herself to the door in a car, if you please. Though I will say that time she Gave Me Something. Well, she couldn't do anything else, really, could she? All tarted up like that. It wasn't much, but it was something. When I think of all those years I worked like a galley-slave to keep her. But I was going to tell you—that last time she came to see me she told me she was going to get married."

"Really?"

"I remember it as though it was yesterday. I was lying down at the time, tired out, I was. I felt as though I should never be able to get up again. Suddenly there's a rat-tat on the door to make my heart jump. I went out and there she was with a posh motor car standing by the kerb. 'Whatever is it now?' I said. 'Don't you know I have to rest in the afternoon?' So she gave me this Little Bit she'd brought for me and we came in here and sat down. I was glad to, I can tell you. I'd been on my feet all the morning. So then she tells me. 'I'm getting married,' she says. 'Whoever to?' I asked. 'Him at the music shop?' 'No,' she said, 'don't be silly. He's married and got two kids. No, this is someone quite different.'"

"Did she mention his name?" Carolus had to ask.

"She called him 'Steve', that's all. It was Steve This and Steve That till I thought I'd have a headache."

"Did she tell you anything about him?"

"Not much. To tell you the truth, I was too tired to ask a lot of questions. Only that he was to do with horse-racing."

"You say this was a month or two ago. Can you be a little more accurate, Mrs Tukes?"

"No, I can't. I can't go racking my brains trying to remember things. It would be too much for me altogether, after a day like today's been. All I remember was some-one had just died in the house where she was living. I remember that, because I couldn't help thinking I wasn't far off it myself, with these stairs to climb every time I go up to bed."

"Oh, this was after Mrs Mallister's death?"

"Yes, I think that was the name. Sonia had been quite friendly with her towards the end, and she went off sudden with her heart, same as any of us might do. I remember Sonia told me."

"Thank you. That dates it exactly."

"I went down to Sonia's funeral," sighed Mrs Tukes. "Well, I couldn't do other, could I, though it was nearly the death of me. I wouldn't do it again, mind you, who-ever was to die. I got back here like a fish on a slab, thinking I was breathing my last. That travelling! Never again! My feet were swollen up for weeks afterwards, and my varicose veins looked like a map of the war. I couldn't get up for two days. Still, I had to Show my Respect. She had no one else to, being an orphan."

"How do you account for her death, Mrs Tukes?"

"It doesn't bear thinking about, does it? It made me quite dizzy to see the place. I can't believe she did it with a purpose, but then you never know. People are funny. The only thing I can think of is that it was a naxident."

"Was she ever subject to vertigo?"

"Dizziness and that? Not that I know of. It was me suffered from dizziness, and do still if I move about too much. She was as healthy as could be. I saw to that, the way I brought her up. The best of everything she had as a little girl, though I had to nearly kill myself working for her. Never had a day's illness in her life that I ever heard of. Still, she might have toppled over, mightn't she?"

"She might. She didn't tell you anything, that time she came to see you, about her life at Cat's Cradle?"

"What sort of thing?"

"Money, or anything like that?"

"She wouldn't talk about money to me. She was too ashamed, after all I'd done for her. She just gave me this little present, in notes, it was, and said no more."

"She didn't seem worried?"

"No. But then she never was a one to worry. It was me did the worrying—she just enjoyed herself."

"She didn't by any chance suggest your looking after some papers for her?"

"Whatever are you getting at? No, she never said any such thing. All she talked about was getting married and this Steve."

Carolus rose. But it seemed that Mrs Tukes was not anxious to end a conversation which, she had first foreseen, would tire her out.

"There was one other thing she said," she gasped, "that afternoon she came to see me. I thought it was funny at the time. She seemed to be talking quite sarcastic. 'You know, auntie dear,' she said, though she scarcely ever called me 'auntie' and never said 'auntie dear' in her life, 'there are people who take me for a fool.' I thought she was getting at me, so I said: 'I'm sure I've never taken you for a fool, Sonia, whatever else I've taken you for.' 'Not *you*,' she said. 'Someone else. But thanks to your careful upbringing, I'm not such a fool as they think. They'll have to come crawling on their knees before I give in. And then it won't be for nothing.' I didn't like the sound of that. 'You be careful,' I said. 'If I can't be good,' she said, and went out to her car and drove off. Funny, wasn't it?"

"No," said Carolus seriously. "It wasn't funny, Mrs Tukes. Goodbye and thank you. You've told me more than you know. In fact, I may say you've told me everything."

"You mean you know how she died?"

"I know why she died," said Carolus. "That's better still."

12

THE Academics was one of those clubs—all *décor* and *ambience*, a single vast flower arrangement and a young man called Peter who never stopped improvising on the piano. But the customers looked tougher and more prosperous than at most similar clubs, bluff and beefy characters, bookmakers or wine-merchants, Carolus thought, mostly accompanied by very young men. He went through the farce of becoming a member, giving Steve Lawson's name as that of his sponsor. He could not have done better, for it brought the tall, youngish, but rather raddled club-owner from behind the bar.

"I'm Gerry Somerset," he said, taking the chair next to Carolus. "I hear you're a friend of Steve Lawson's."

"An acquaintance, yes," said Carolus.

"You don't know him well then?"

"Not very, I'm afraid. Why?"

"He owes us a lot of money," said Mr Somerset. "More than we can afford to lose."

"I've always understood he was very well off," said Carolus.

"So have I!" exclaimed Mr Somerset. "Everybody thought so. I mean, his car and clothes and everything. He always *seemed* to have plenty of money, too. Spent quite a lot. He had that *way* about him, as though he was very rich. Everyone thought so."

"And isn't he?"

"My dear, he owes money to *everyone*. Many of my best customers. Then there's that horse he's supposed to own."

"He doesn't?"

"No one knows who owns it with the number of half-shares he has sold in the poor beast. Cyril Nutt-Campion talked of going to the police about it, but I persuaded him not to. I didn't want anything to do with Miss Law. But Cecil Waveney-Long—that's him over there with that very good-looking boy—says that he doesn't see why Steve Lawson should get away with it. Well, nor do I, if it comes to that."

"You have his address?"

"Oh yes. Cat's Cradle, Somewhere-or-Other. In fact Adrian Stokes-Grey talks of going down there to see if he can get anything back. Everyone wants him to."

"You knew there was a possibility of his getting married, didn't you?"

"Not that piece with the music shop? He brought her here a couple of times. I thought she was common." Carolus did not say that, common or not, she was dead, but thinking it time he asked a question, he said: "What is known about Lawson?"

"Nothing, really, when it comes to it. That's what everyone said when it began to look peculiar—we don't really know anything. Except what he said, of course, and you can't take any notice of that. I mean you hear so much. He said he was at Harrow College but Ronnie Bright-Wilson looked him up in a book somewhere and said his name wasn't there. When he asked Steve about it, he said he meant Wellington School. So what can you say?"

"Nothing, I'm afraid."

"Then he was supposed to be coming into all this money from somebody who'd died. I forget how many thousand pounds it was. He told everyone about that. But we never heard any more of it."

"When did he tell you this?"

"The last time he was here. About a month ago, I should think."

"How long have you known him?"

"Well, he's been *about* for ages. Lionel Stone-Richards used to know him when he lived in London four or five years ago. He says Steve had plenty of money then. So you don't know what to think, do you?"

"Yes," said Carolus. "I think he made or came into a good deal of money once and has done what plenty of others have done—got through it."

"I suppose that must be it. Everyone liked him till this happened. I was hoping when you gave his name you'd be able to tell us something about him."

Carolus did not say that the hope had been mutual. He finished his drink and went out to return to his club for the night. He felt he had done pretty well so far. If his other potential informants were as obliging, he would soon be able to return to Cat's Cradle.

He made three telephone calls next morning. Mr Arthur Picknet, the solicitor whose name Mallister had given as a reference, regretted that he could not see Carolus. He was far too busy. But he could say there and then on the telephone that he had known James Mallister for many years and had always found him punctiliously honest. If it was a matter of credit or a contract or hire-purchase agreement, he had no hesitation in saying that from his knowledge of Mallister the utmost confidence could be placed in his word. He, Mr Picknet, could not actually underwrite such a contract; it was against his principles. But he could recommend it.

Carolus tried to explain that it was a more personal matter and again asked for a few minutes of Mr Picknet's time.

"Quite impossible, I'm afraid," he was told. "I simply haven't a moment. A client is waiting to see me now. But I've always found Mallister a splendid fellow. Sad about his wife. Long expected though, I believe. Yes, Mallister's as sound as a bell."

"Thank . . ." Carolus began, but the receiver was put down.

He resolved not to give the Reverend Ralph Cracknell the same opportunity. He phoned his address in the suburb of Grange Hill, and was answered by a jolly voice saying, "Hallo-o! "

"Mr Cracknell? "

"In person! " called the voice with a chuckle.

"My name is Deene. I wondered if you would be kind enough to let me call on you? There is something I should like to discuss."

"What's the nature of the complaint? "

Should he say ' Murder! ' and see if that did away with the chuckle? No, he wanted his interview.

" It's a personal matter. I'd rather not discuss it on the phone."

" Quite. Where are you speaking from? Or should I say ' whence-'? "

Carolus gave the name of his club.

" Ah-ha. And you want to come out here and see me? "

" If I may. This afternoon, perhaps? "

" Let's see. Yes! About four? "

Carolus was about to take his leave when he heard the chuckle again.

" Don't bring the Chapter with you, will you, Mr Deene? "

This, he thought, will be hard going.

Mrs Cremoine Rose's telephone was engaged continuously for the next three-quarters of an hour, but he eventually got through.

" Ye-es? " said a rich but dubious voice.

Carolus explained that he was staying at Cat's Cradle.

" That tr-ragic name! " said Mrs Rose.

" For you, yes, I'm afraid it must be," said Carolus. " I am sure you don't wish to be reminded of it. But the truth is, Mrs Rose, there are one or two things I feel you ought to know."

" Really? Concerning? "

" It is a little hard to explain this on the phone. Perhaps I could see you? "

" Who, exactly, are you? " asked Mrs Rose reasonably enough.

" I'm afraid I shall seem to you a very interfering sort of person. I'm a guest in the house who has gone to live there since your sister's death. Mrs Derosse, the proprietress, gave me your name and address."

" This is all very irregular," said Mrs Rose.

" I'm sorry . . ."

" I shall see you. Whether or not my solicitor will be present, I shall decide in the meantime. You may come here at 12.30 this morning. I will give you ten minutes."

" That's in an hour's time? "

" Precisely."

Carolus began to feel he had congratulated himself too soon. Mr Cracknell's jokes and Mrs Rose's grandeur would not be easy to bear. But he fortified himself with a whisky-and-soda and set off for Alexandra Gate.

The house had an entrance so expensive-looking and decorative that he could not at first find the electric bell. Topiaric shrubs in the shape of peacocks grew in pale-green tubs bound with burnished copper, ships' lanterns hung on wrought-iron brackets above them, a ship's bell on a more elaborately wrought-iron bracket was there, the knocker was a lion's head, the letter box a slit in a piece of cut and shining brass. But when the green front door opened the splendour temporarily vanished because it revealed a fussy and untidy char.

" Yes, you're to come in," she said. " Mrs Rose is in the drawing-room on the first floor."

She was indeed. She rose majestically from a study of *Vogue* and pointed to an armchair. The room was heavily perfumed and furnished with baroque profusion.

" I am ready to hear what you have to tell me," announced Mrs Rose, a fine fleshy woman in mustard yellow.

Carolus had a feeling that in spite of all this *montage,* frankness would pay him best.

" You won't like it, I'm afraid. I'm that most tiresome of beings, a private investigator. Worse still, I do it because I like doing it."

" Do what? " asked Mrs Rose, haughtily but not impatiently.

"I suppose I must call it investigate. I get consulted by people when there is anything that seems inexplicable about a death."

"Was there anything that seemed inexplicable about my sister's death?"

"Well, it gave rise to a great deal of speculation."

"I can't think why. She was warned that she hadn't long to live and the doctor was satisfied that she died naturally."

"I know. But for some reason the members of that household began behaving in a curious way after it. There was a great deal of suspicion and talk among them."

"I can scarcely be held responsible for that."

"Certainly not. Your sister's will was much discussed."

"I'm not surprised. It was a most questionable will. That Grissell woman! And all that money to the servants!"

"Her husband was cut out."

"For no adequate reason known to me. I still cannot see . . ."

"Did you know there had since been another death in the house?"

"I read it in the newspapers. What of it?"

"Mrs Rose, let me appeal to you. I'm really trying to find the truth in a highly anomalous situation. I admit that there is no apparent connection between your sister's death and Sonia Reid's. But you would be helping me enormously if you would tell me a little about your sister and her husband. Strictly between ourselves, I mean."

Mrs Rose blinked, then said unexpectedly: "Have a glass of champagne?"

"Thank you."

Carolus watched her go majestically to the door and bring in a tray which had been set on a table on the landing. There was an ice bucket containing a bottle and two glasses. As she poured out, he noticed it was Veuve Clicquot.

"I don't see why not," said Mrs Rose when she had sipped. Carolus realized that she was answering his appeal. "You appear to be a gentleman." Carolus waited. "My sister and I were the only children. My father's name was Dodgham."

Carolus couldn't resist this solemn announcement though his idiotic question might have cost him his information. "Did he make cars?" he asked.

"I don't know what you mean. It is spelt D-o-d-g-h-a-m. My father was a well-known musical entrepreneur. My sister and I were brought up to play several instruments. Until my marriage I occasionally performed at charity concerns. The harp."

Carolus nodded eagerly.

"We married in the same year, but very differently. Lydia married a worthy but insignificant man. I, as you doubtless know, married Otto Cremoine Rose, who has been referred to in the press as a Take-Over Tycoon. Lydia's marriage was not as unfortunate as it might have been, for we both had adequate private fortunes.

"I do not believe that James Mallister's motive was the sordid one of money. For some years he and Lydia were a devoted couple, but, when she became an invalid, she lost her happy disposition. She was, I am afraid, an embittered woman. Another glass of champagne?"

"Thank you. I gathered that in your sister's last months she resented her husband's association with a young woman who lived in the house?"

"I visited her a week or two before she died. Her attitude, I thought, was shocking. She spoke of her husband in a derisory manner, not as if she was troubled by the association you mention, but as though it was beneath contempt. She told me then she had cut him out of her will, but did not say that she had left a large sum to Miss Grissell."

"They were at school together, I believe."

"They were. I was, of course, considerably younger and remember Grissell as a senior girl, a bullying and cruel creature whom I detested. Then who are these Jerrisons?"

"A man and woman who work at Cat's Cradle."

"I know that. Why were they so lavishly endowed? My sister must have been crazy."

"Do you mean that?"

"I do. There has been madness in the family, just as there is hereditary heart disease. I am thankful I am untouched by both. More champagne?"

"If you really think that her long illness had weakened your sister's mind . . ."

"But of course. Isn't that well known to you all? She was far from being mentally normal when I saw her. Grumbling because her husband, a frail-looking man more often ill than she was at first, was fit enough to watch her die. Grumbling because he came to crow over her and grumbling because he didn't spend enough time with her. She seemed to be angry with everyone in that house, the proprietress, the other guests, even that over-bearing Grissell. And suspicious. She told me quite seriously she thought she was being poisoned."

"Really? This is most interesting. Whom did she suspect?"

"All and sundry, so far as I could gather. No one in particular."

"Not even her husband?"

"I think not. James had just gone into a hospital for an operation; the only person in the house of whom she spoke at all pleasantly was the girl who has since died, Sonia Reid. It appeared that a friendship had grown up between them. They discussed music and Lydia had ordered a most elaborate record-player from the girl's shop. Hi-Fi she called it. It gave her some consolation in her last weeks. Yet there was no mention of this Sonia Reid in her will, the last version of which was made after their friendship had sprung up."

"You remained on intimate terms with your sister, Mrs Rose?"

"Not very, I fear. There was, I am sorry to say, a tendency on her part to be jealous as my husband's status in the nation's finances became more and more prominently mentioned in the press, while James Mallister remained a bank-clerk. It was natural enough, perhaps, particularly when she was well enough to come up to town and we could not always include her husband and her in our lists of guests."

"You entertain a good deal?"

Mrs Rose stared at him.

"You surely must know . . . must have read . . ." She seemed genuinely perplexed.

"I'm afraid I don't follow that sort of thing."

His hostess seemed affronted.

"I can scarcely believe that anyone could remain unaware . . . However, we will let that pass. I think I have answered your question. Is there any other assistance I can give you?"

"You, personally, have no doubt that your sister's death was due to natural causes?"

"None. It has been attested by a competent physician."

"You don't think that her heart attack could have been induced in some way?"

"That is a most unpleasant thought. I shall refuse to harbour it. Who would be so wicked and take such a serious risk when it was known that my sister could not live long in any case?"

"That's certainly a point. I gather that no one in the house knew that she had recently changed her will."

"You see? Frankly, Mr Deene, I think you are trying to stir up muddy waters. If there had been the slightest doubt at the time, surely there would have been a post-mortem and an inquest? I know very little about such things."

"There was no doubt at the time. It is the result of what has happened since."

"You cannot be suggesting that the case may be re-opened in some way?"

"I'm not in the confidence of the police. I shouldn't think it's impossible, though."

"Then I shall ask my husband to intervene immediately."

"I'm afraid that would not help very much. In England, Mrs Rose, there are limits to the powers of even a Take-Over Tycoon."

She seemed to contemplate this statement then dismiss it as preposterous.

"Another glass of champagne?" she suggested with her lavish smile. It was gruesomely well rehearsed. Carolus could well believe that she was accustomed to entertaining.

13

THE Reverend Ralph Cracknell was as cheerful as he had sounded on the phone. He came to the door of his bright little house, a plump and smiling man of fifty.

"What a punctual person!" he said. "Punctuality's

next to godliness in my opinion. Come along in. This isn't a vicarage because I'm not a vicar. I'm the curate-in-charge of St Aug's round the corner, so I suppose this is the curate-in-chargery."

" St Aug's? " Carolus could not help asking.

" St Augustine's. Only it sounds so august. Like a cupper? "

" Thank you."

" It's just being made. My crone will bring it. Squattez, and let's hear your trouble."

Carolus decided to get this over as quickly as he could.

" Do you know Bishop Grissell? "

" Know him? Known him for thirty years. We were at St Mick's together. Beg your pardon. St Michael's Theological College. What about him? "

" I'm investigating the deaths of two women in the house in which Bishop Grissell lives."

" Whe-whee-ew! " whistled Mr Cracknell. " Not *again*? "

" Again? "

" Oh nothing. So poor old Grissell's got involved in a murder case? "

" Why did you say ' again ', Mr Cracknell? "

" You know how one says things. Tell me about the murders."

" I haven't said there has been a murder, and certainly not that Bishop Grissell is involved in one. I said he lived in the house."

Mr Cracknell turned to Carolus sharply, though still smiling. " Then why come to me, if Grissell's not involved? "

" Just that I found myself working in mid-air. I knew nothing about the people in the guest-house in which these things had happened. It was necessary to learn what I could, and your name was given me as that of a friend of Bishop Grissell who might be helpful."

"Helpful to you or to him? That's the question."

"One hopes it is the same thing," said Carolus priggishly. "But it is the truth we want, Mr Cracknell."

"Tell me, how deep is old Grissell in this? Up to the neck, I suppose? He has a gift for being in the wrong place at the wrong time, getting off on the wrong foot, and then putting it in it, his foot I mean. But seriously, you can leave him off your list of suspects. He may have made his blunders, but he would never hurt a woman. Not a white woman, anyway."

Instead of seizing on the last five words, Carolus said: "Tell me a little about him."

"Old Grissell? Vigorous chap. Strong as a horse as a young man. Used to do feats of strength at St Mick's. No one was surprised when he decided on missionary work. It was a bit of a joke at St Mick's. Cannibals would be in the cooking-pot, we said, while the missionary did the war dance. Ever hear him preach?"

"No."

"It's worth hearing. That terrific deep voice of his. Like someone out of the Old Testament. And his sister's a real trouper, too. Those two went off to darkest Africa and we were sorry for anyone who might oppose them. He was out there twenty-four years."

"Did you see much of him during that time?"

"He came home on leave once or twice. Always looked me up. Or rather looked me down, as you might say. I've never been ambitious, you see. Not very pop with the high-ups. They find me too frivolous, I fear. So, as old Grissell became more and more important, I paddled along quietly. I believe I am in for promotion now, but I've never looked for it. Old Grissell was all for a bishopric and, my word, he got it. Colonial, of course, but still. She was just the same. Knew how to get what she wanted.

I hear she has just come into a large sum of money from an old school friend. That sounds typical."

"The old school friend was one of the two women whose deaths I am investigating," said Carolus, and left this to sink in.

"I say, you're not suggesting . . . No, that's impossible. I don't mind a laugh at the Grissells' expense, but really . . ."

Carolus said nothing.

"Of course, he has a temper," admitted Mr Cracknell.

"Yes?"

"Violent, when it's roused. He threw old Figgley in the duckpond at St Mick's. Picked him up bodily and threw him right in. Figgley's Bishop of Hatfield now. He was no weakling himself, but Grissell was in a towering rage. Figgley had called him a gorilla. He did look rather like one as a young man."

"Bishop Grissell retired early," said Carolus.

"Yes," said Mr Cracknell thoughtfully. "He did."

"Any particular reason?"

"You don't know?" asked Mr Cracknell rather slyly. "I thought everyone knew that."

Carolus shook his head.

"I don't want to rake up that old story," said Cracknell. "It was all very unfortunate and has been long forgotten now. Most unfair, I thought at the time."

"Something that happened in Africa?"

"Oh yes! It couldn't have happened here, of course. That temper of his. It concerned a house-boy of his. Died in hospital. The doctors proved he couldn't have lived long, anyway. But it appeared that poor old Grissell had lost his temper with the boy. All most unfortunate. And of course all the relatives and friends made a tremendous fuss. Half the tribe turned up at the inquiry. Grissell's name was cleared. Completely cleared. But it was felt best that he should find another field for his endeavours and he retired to England. These things happen. Ah, here's the char. Sugar and milk? "

" Thanks. What year was this? "

" About five years ago. You won't find anything in the newspapers at the time. It was kept out of them. Prestige and so on. Mind you, I've always liked Grissell. He's not the most generous of men, but his heart's in the right place. Funny, he was never given a nickname at St Mick's. Perhaps because his own name rather fitted. Figgley was Figgs and I, of course, was Crackers, but no one ever thought of calling him by anything but his correct name. Does that mean something or doesn't it? "

" Not necessarily, I think. He could afford to retire? "

" Oh yes. Private money. Quite well off, I believe. Wish I were. You'll give him my salaams, won't you? Say old Crackers wants to be remembered to him."

" I don't think I shall mention that I've met you," said Carolus.

" Best not, perhaps. I shouldn't want him to think I'd been taking his name in vain. Or his sister's. Phiz is a bit of a terror, isn't she? "

" She's certainly very blunt. When did you see the Grissells last? "

" When they first came home. They popped down here for a week-end. I got him to preach at St Aug's. Rather hair-raising, really. He seemed to take my parishioners for the heathen. Hell-fire, you know, and retribution. One old lady fainted. The choir thought it no end of a lark, but I expect they think the same of me."

When Carolus left Mr Cracknell it was past five o'clock, but he decided to try to finish his roster in order to reach Cat's Cradle at lunchtime on the following day.

He had only one more call—Conway Towers Preparatory School, at which the Jerrisons had been employed.

This was at Orbiton, a reputedly healthy suburb on the hills, not more than twenty miles away but by a different route crossing the main roads into London. He decided not to phone the school before going there, though he realized that during the summer holidays it might be deserted, even by the proprietor, Mr Colin Topham.

He found it to be one of those large Victorian mansions built for rich city men in the sixties and seventies of the last century. He asked for the headmaster and was shown into a room which, from his own days as a small boy at a preparatory school, he recognized as 'the study'. He had not long to look about him, however, for a small man in white flannels and a blazer burst into the room and addressed him irritably.

"I'm not seeing applicants until tomorrow," he said. "The agents should have told you that. Have you got a degree?"

"Yes," said Carolus mildly.

"What is it?"

"Honours History."

"University?"

"Oxford."

"College?"

"Christ Church."

"School?"

"Beaumont."

Mr Topham looked aggrieved.

"I was playing tennis," he said. "I told the agents not to send anyone before tomorrow." He strolled to the window. "Is that your car out there?"

"Yes."

"Teach for a hobby, do you?"

"Yes."

"I don't know whether I want anything like that at Conway Towers. The last man who said it was his hobby made it too much of a hobby altogether. He had to go in the middle of a term. Any athletic distinctions? "

" I got a half blue for boxing."

" War service? "

" Commandos."

" Hm. I don't think it would do at all. The other men wouldn't like it. They haven't got degrees, you see. My senior assistant has no qualifications on paper, but he's been with me eighteen years. He'd feel slighted, I think. I wanted a younger man. What brought you here, Mr . . ."

" Deene. I wanted to see you. To ask one or two questions."

" Questions? Oh, I can see it would never do. Never. We are at cross-purposes already. I don't expect an applicant to ask questions. It's an excellent post. Three hundred pounds a year with board and residence."

It had to end, though Carolus regretted the necessity. " I did not come to apply for a post on your staff," he said gently.

" You didn't? Then what on earth did you come for? I was in the middle of a set of tennis. I understood you were an applicant." Mr Topham's face suddenly changed and an ingratiating smile spread over it. "Perhaps you are a prospective parent? I mean, perhaps you thought of entering your son? "

" No. I wanted to ask you about some people called Jerrison."

Mr Topham looked disappointed, flustered but, most of all, baffled.

" Jerrison? Parents of mine? "

" No, they . . ."

" They weren't those people who came to see me about young Foley, were they? Said they were his uncle and aunt? I had to phone Foley's parents, I remember, who said that on *no* account . . . No, they gave their name as Jeromé. I can't call to mind any Jerrisons."

"They were on your staff," put in Carolus sharply, but, as he saw too soon, ambiguously.

"On the staff? I've only had married couples twice. Both failures. Either the man has no discipline or the wife quarrels with Matron. Besides, a woman can't very well Take Games. It doesn't do. Now let's think. One of these couples was called Packham, so it can't be them . . . they . . . those. It must be the others. They were here more recently. Only stayed a term. Most unpleasant. The man called my senior assistant an old shellback. And the woman was a virago. Nothing less. She actually set about the Matron in front of some of the boys. I'm sorry to say they cheered. Most unseemly. It was soon round the school. Unluckily Matron suffered a small disfigure-ment for some days. A black eye, in fact. But you, who know how boys behave, will guess what impertinence this led to. 'Oh Matron, what a beauty! ' That sort of thing. Fortunately it did not reach the parents' ears, as these people were leaving, anyway. It must be these you are inquiring about. I can tell you at once—don't employ them. Better introduce a herd of wild buffalo into your school. When I paid the man, he walked out of my study singing the harvest hymn. You know—' All is safely gathered in '. Can you imagine it? "

"Yes. But the Jerrisons were not on your teaching staff. They worked in the house."

Light dawned.

"Oh, the *Jerrisons*! " said Mr Topham. "Of course. They're not thinking of returning to us? " he asked hope-fully.

"I've no reason to suppose so."

"Pity, that. The only time my wife was free of domestic troubles was while they were with us. Excellent people, excellent. Even Matron admitted it, though she did complain that Mrs Jerrison was inclined to gossip. As I told my wife, that, coming from Matron, was . . . but never mind, they were the best servants we have ever employed."

" Why did they leave you? " asked Carolus.

" Oh *that*! Most unfortunate, really. My wife is very meticulous about quantities, you see. She likes to measure things out herself. Sugar, tea, mar . . . butter, bacon and so on. Absolutely necessary in catering, as we do, for fifty-odd boys and a staff of eight. Through long experience my wife knows just the quantities. They are generous without being prodigal. But it seemed that this did not accord with Mrs Jerrison's ideas. There was some heated discussion concerning tea in the kitchen and cocoa at night. I forget the details. Tempers rose, however, and unfortunately Mrs Jerrison, who had been a treasure till then, used the word 'stingy'. That was enough for my wife. She insisted that, treasure or no treasure, Mrs Jerrison must go. I tried to intervene. Matron did her best, but it seemed to add fuel to the flames. A tragedy, really."

" Did you know anything about them before they came to you? "

"Oh yes. Unexceptionable references. He had a fine army record. She had been a sergeant in the WRAF. Their conduct was faultless until that distressing scene."

" And since? "

" Ah, since. Yes, we did learn something. My senior assistant, a first-rate fellow, has one small weakness. He cannot resist a flutter. He follows horse-racing—avidly. It is his Achilles heel. I have had to mention it before now. There was an ominous silence from his classroom during the first period in the morning and I found that his boys were set to write an essay while he studied 'form', as he called it. While Jerrison was here, this was greatly intensified. They apparently formed a co-operative. Undignified in a member of the teaching staff, as I told Breechman. But highly successful, I gathered. My senior assistant did not come to me for a single advance of salary that term. After the Jerrisons left there was an attempt to continue this by correspondence, so we learned where they were employed. They went straight from us to a seaside guest-house called Cat's Cradle."

"Yes. I'm staying there."

"Are you thinking of employing the Jerrisons?"

"No. I'm investigating two deaths in the house."

Mr Topham winced. "I thought you said you were a schoolmaster?"

"I am. In term-time. But we all have our holiday relaxations. Yours, I see, is tennis."

"You mean I have been called in from a very exciting set to assist in some kind of amateur investigation?"

"Two women have died rather mysteriously."

Mr Topham began to splutter. "This is really too much," he said. "I am not interested in mysterious deaths in guest-houses."

"You see, you employed the Jerrisons. You were our only link with their past."

"I will not be called a link!" said Mr Topham angrily. Then added more calmly. "Are the Jerrisons suspected?"

"Of what?"

"Of anything. You say there have been two deaths."

"I don't know whom the police suspect, or whether they have any suspicions. I wanted to know anything I could about the people in the house."

"So you drive up here posing as an applicant for a place on my staff, interrupt my well-earned relaxation and, saying you are a schoolmaster, ask me questions about a housekeeper and her husband we employed some years ago. I am glad I have told you nothing."

"On the contrary, you have told me a great deal. I'm most grateful to you."

Mr Topham made an explosive sound and showed Carolus out, not for the sake of politeness but as though he could not trust him alone in the entrance-hall.

14

DURING the few days after his return to Cat's Cradle, Carolus learned just what Helena had meant by an atmosphere of threatening stillness before a storm. For one thing, the weather, incredibly, remained hot and humid, though it was now well into September and everyone kept saying it couldn't last. For another thing, Miss Grey, who had never had a day's illness since coming to Cat's Cradle, complained of headaches and sleeplessness and said she was afraid the place was getting on her nerves.

"I don't know what to do," Mrs Derosse confided in Carolus. "It sounds an awful thing to say, but when that happened to Sonia I thought at least it would mean the end of all this. Two deaths within two months—surely nothing else could happen. I thought, when they'd got over the tragedy of Sonia, people would be themselves again. But no. Steve Lawson walks about like a lion in a cage. He won't speak to anyone and looks as though he'd kill you as soon as look at you. He hasn't paid his bill for weeks, now. Even Mr Mallister, who has been quite a sheet-anchor all through it, keeping so calm about everything, has begun to get nervy. Now there are these headaches of Miss Grey's."

"I thought your niece was a stand-by for you," said Carolus.

"She means well, Mr Deene, but it seems to be getting beyond her. Mrs Natterley complained of someone walking about outside her room last night, though I'm sure it's just her imagination. My niece is very able and a good friend to me, but there's not much she can do. She keeps saying she has a plan which will clear it all up but, after all, she came before poor Sonia died and she wasn't able to prevent that. I do wish you'd find out what is wrong, Mr Deene. Mrs Gort says you're so clever at that and it's really terrible to go on like this. Haven't you any notion about it?"

"Yes. I have. I think one or perhaps several of your guests or staff are holding back information which they ought to have given to the police."

Mrs Derosse looked distressed.

"Really? Oh, I should hardly think that. The police questioned us all very thoroughly. Have you anyone in mind?"

"Not yet. I hope I shall know in time. Mrs Derosse, was it your custom to visit Mrs Mallister's room from time to time when she was ill?"

"Of course. Several times a day. I usually saw her after meals to know that everything was all right. She never lost her appetite, you know."

"When did you see her for the last time?"

Carolus thought there was a shade of confusion on her face.

"The day she died. Just after tea."

"She had dinner that evening?"

"Very little. She told Mrs Jerrison she wasn't hungry. I sent up some turbot, I remember."

"You didn't go up afterwards?"

"Not that evening. I was very busy downstairs."

"Let's see, whose room is next to hers?"

This time Mrs Derosse looked uncomfortable. "Her room was on the corner. There is only one room adjoining it, really, that occupied by Miss Godwin and Miss Grey."

"You don't know who did visit Lydia Mallister that last evening?"

"Miss Grissell nearly always went. Yes, I think she said at the inquest that she had been to see her."

"When would be a good time to catch Miss Grissell?"

"When she comes in from her walk. She goes out most mornings about ten for a walk along the cliffs. She's usually back at midday."

Carolus saw Phiz coming up the drive. She wore the kind of tweeds that led you to expect dogs at her heels, but there were none. That was the trouble with Phiz, Carolus reflected, she just missed her type. She looked like a woman missionary who had braved hardship and danger, but her petulant rudeness and self-opinionated vulgarity did not belong to those heroic women at all. She was a misfit, and, Carolus thought, a very unhappy woman.

"Good morning," Carolus said as she approached.

"Hullo! Snooping?" she asked.

"Yes. Hard. Where *were* you on the night of the crime, Miss Grissell?"

"Is that meant to be funny?"

"Not at all. I'd like to know. I mean on both nights on which a woman died. Did you, for instance, see Lydia Mallister that night?"

Phiz gave a snort which was meant to express amusement. "I think you've got a nerve to ask me questions, but on the other hand I've got nothing, of course, to hide. Yes, I went to see Lydia as usual. After dinner."

"And was the visit—was she 'as usual'?"

"Not in the least. She talked in a very odd way. Seemed to have forgotten our long friendship going back to school. Bitter and not very friendly. I've got no patience with that sort of thing. Told her that, ill or not ill, what she needed was a dose of salts. She gave a superior sort of smile to that and asked me if I thought I was still a school-monitor."

"Dear, dear," said Carolus, managing to look quite serious.

"She talked about that idiotic sister of hers. Pretentious, ridiculous woman. Remember her as a whining child. Lydia pretended that evening to feel some affection for her. I knew *that* to be hypocrisy. Meant to annoy me. Forgive most things to an invalid, but not that sort of humbug. 'Why don't you get her to come and see you?' I asked. 'It's too late for that.' 'Don't be absurd, Lydia,' I said. 'You may live a long time yet.' She answered quite calmly, but with a sharp undertone which I didn't like. 'No,' she said. 'You won't have to wait long now.' 'Wait?' I said. 'Well, aren't you waiting?' she asked. 'You know I've left you something; you were always fond of money.' This was too much, and I told her I had no expectations from her and shouldn't wish to have any. Curious, because she *had* left me money. Quite a large sum. Only to spite her husband, though."

"You really think that?"

"Sure of it. She had cut James Mallister out and had to dispose of the money somehow. Towards the end she had no affection for anyone but herself."

"You are very hard on her memory, Miss Grissell."

"I knew her. Knew her for forty years. Don't blame her for cutting out her husband. Running round with that dreadful Welton woman."

"I think they are sincerely fond of one another."

The sound which 'Phiz my dear' made this time was something more than a snort, though rather less than a bellow.

"Fond? That woman is fond of whatever suits her. When we first came here she tried . . . she made attempts . . . she actually set her cap at my brother. I watched it. My brother, of course, soon showed her that he was not to be inveigled." The bishop came towards them. "Telling him about the Welton woman," said Phiz.

"Oh that! I think my sister read more into it than was there. But I must say frankly neither of us trusts those two."

"Which two?"

It was Phiz who answered, using only the most hostile surnames. "Welton and Mallister," she said. "You can be sure that, if there was anything irregular about the death of Lydia, those two had a hand in it. They didn't know Mallister had been cut out of Lydia's will."

"That's a very grave suggestion," said Carolus.

"I speak my mind," retorted Phiz. "And I don't care who knows it."

"My sister carries frankness to a degree at which, as I tell her, it becomes indiscreet," apologized the bishop.

"Time someone spoke," said Phiz. "Can't see people murdered and stand by doing nothing."

"Did you see someone murdered?"

"Not actually. Almost as good as."

"Perhaps you suspect James Mallister and Esmée Welton of having something to do with Sonia Reid's death?"

"No. That was obvious."

"I think, Phiz my dear, that you had better say no more," said the bishop anxiously.

"Unless, of course, you have some concrete evidence, when you should certainly give it to the police."

Miss Grissell's snort was mild this time, as though from the depths of a feeding-bag. "I've the evidence of my own common sense," she declared.

Realizing that he had reached a dead end, Carolus made an excuse to leave them.

After lunch he had an opportunity of approaching Miss Godwin and Miss Grey, though not as he would have liked, separately. They sat with their eternal tatting in a corner of the lounge, which was just then deserted. They smiled their permission for him to join them but, when he tried to turn the conversation on the events he was investigating, they were at first severely uncommunicative.

"I couldn't possibly discuss these things," said Miss Godwin. "My friend Miss Grey is already suffering from sleeplessness on account of them."

"Wouldn't it be better, then, if they could be cleared up? You see, Miss Godwin, you have the room next to the one in which Lydia Mallister died."

"What of it?" asked Miss Godwin truculently.

"I feel that, if you cast your mind back, there might be something about that evening you remember."

Carolus was surprised to find her eyeing him rather suspiciously.

"How could there be?" she asked. Then, more secretively, "Have you examined the bedrooms of this house?"

"Oh yes," said Carolus.

"The cupboards?"

"Of course."

"You *know* then?"

Carolus decided to take a chance.

"Yes," he answered.

Miss Godwin and Miss Grey exchanged glances.

"Tell him all," said Miss Grey. "It will be a relief."

Miss Godwin hesitated a moment, then said: "The cupboards are built-in, as you have seen; the walls are thick, but the cupboard in our room has only a thin partition between it and Mrs Mallister's room. You saw that?"

Carolus nodded.

"We listened," whispered Miss Grey.

"Not deliberately, of course," said Miss Godwin.

"Well, not at first," qualified Miss Grey.

"My friend Miss Grey and I have felt most uncomfortable about it. You see we heard things which might be . . . relevant. We have felt we ought to speak to the authorities, but naturally we didn't like to. It is a relief to be able to tell this to someone . . . a gentleman, who will treat it with discretion."

Carolus was too experienced to suppose that he was about to have his problem neatly solved for him. But, to say the least of it, he was interested, until Miss Godwin continued dampingly: "My friend Miss Grey and I could not hear many actual words," she admitted. "But the drift of the conversation was often plain. That evening, for instance, when Mrs Derosse came to the room . . ."

"At what time?" interrupted Carolus.

"About her usual time. Eight-thirty or nine. Miss Grissell usually called immediately after dinner. Then after a pause Mrs Derosse would arrive. As I was telling you, that evening there were quite loud words between them. I have always found Mrs Derosse the most gentle and amiable of people, but that evening I fear she lost her temper. It was quite distressing. My friend Miss Grey wanted us to intervene, but I dissuaded her."

"You could not gather what had caused it?"

"Early in the discussion I did catch the word 'turbot' but it seemed to go much farther than any petty question of diet. It lasted some ten minutes, after which Mrs Derosse went out, not actually slamming the door, but closing it firmly."

"Are you quite sure this happened on the evening of Mrs Mallister's death?"

"Oh quite. I know, because there had already been some hard words between Lydia Mallister and Miss Grissell, who visited her earlier. Nothing that Lydia said was audible, but Miss Grissell's voice is very penetrating. Very. In fact I heard her make a somewhat indelicate suggestion that evening."

"*Really?*" said the astounded Carolus.

"I scarcely like to repeat it, but she said that what Lydia should do was to take a dose of salts. Later she told Lydia not to be absurd. There was nothing perhaps in that. Miss Grissell is notoriously outspoken and they were old friends. But the quarrel with Mrs Derosse was most unusual."

"Did anyone else visit her that evening?"

"Yes. And this is what has troubled my friend Miss Grey and me. After Mrs Jerrison had come to settle her for the night, *quite* late it must have been, past ten certainly, I suddenly heard Mrs Mallister say, 'There you are, darling!' I had not even heard the door open. Someone had entered secretly, someone whom Lydia was expecting. I *think* I know who it was, but only from the timbre of the voice, really. It was Sonia Reid."

"But that wasn't unusual, was it?"

"At that time of night? Most! And neither my friend Miss Grey nor I heard her go. How long she remained there talking in low tones, we do not know. Then there was a really horrid thing. My friend Miss Grey has never been a good sleeper. She woke in the small hours of that morning. When she looked at her watch it was nearly three o'clock. And she heard "—" I am *almost* certain I heard, dear," interrupted Miss Grey—" the door of Lydia's room being closed very softly, followed by footsteps past our door. She was not troubled by it at the time, Mr Deene. Lydia sometimes needed attention in the night. But since then it has disturbed Miss Grey dreadfully. It accounts for her insomnia, I am sure."

" I'm very glad my friend Miss Godwin has told you," said Miss Grey with a sad smile.

" So am I," said Carolus prosaically. " You have helped me a great deal. Since his return from hospital, James Mallister has occupied that room, I believe."

There was a certain stiffness noticeable in the two old ladies.

" I wonder whether . . ." Carolus began, but Miss Godwin spoke with horrified decisiveness.

" You surely don't suppose, Mr Deene, that my friend Miss Grey and I would allow ourselves to overhear anything from a *man's* room? " she said.

" The cupboard is kept locked," explained Miss Grey more calmly. " And not used except during Mr Mallister's working hours."

Thus reproved, Carolus left them and made his way to his room. He wanted time to sort out the things communicated to him that day.

Late that afternoon he had a talk with Esmée Welton, who came home earlier than Mallister that day. " James will be at the bank till late," she said quietly, as though they were already married. " It's their monthly balance or something—I never know. It happens from time to time. James does not tell me much."

" Doesn't he? "

" About his work, I mean. I'm glad, really. Men who talk about their work are apt to over-do it, I find. Especially when it's something dull like banking."

" I told you I was trying to clear up the . . . mystery that has grown up round his wife's death? "

" I thought you said you were more interested in Sonia's."

" It's impossible not to look for some connection between them."

" I shouldn't have thought there was any. James doesn't, either. I know he has always thought Lydia died naturally."

" And Sonia? "

" We did not know her very well. Just from living in the same house, you know."

" You and she both went into Belstock every day? "

" Yes, but I have my car. Steve Lawson used to take her in his Jaguar. He sold it recently, I believe. Sometimes I gave her a lift back here, if I saw her. But we didn't get on very well."

" Would you mind telling me about the night of her death? "

" Certainly. What little I can. James and I decided to stay in Belstock for dinner that evening. There is quite a good restaurant called the Golden Plover. At least we thought it was quite good. We ate and had coffee and returned to Cat's Cradle in my car about ten. I was feeling awful. It came on suddenly, a terrible sleepiness and sick feeling. No one was about when we came in. I went straight up to bed. James thought it was something I had eaten. I didn't actually vomit, but could scarcely keep my eyes open. You know, that liverish feeling. I knew nothing more till I was awakened by a knocking on my door."

" On *your* door? "

" Yes. It was Christine Derosse and Bishop Grissell. Christine said there had been an accident and they were just going round to see everything was all right. I was still feeling drowsy. 'Any need for me to come?' I asked and she said there wasn't. So I slept till the morning, then came down to hear what had happened."

"So you didn't see Mr Mallister after . . . What time would it be?"

"Not later than ten-thirty when I went up to bed. He told me next day he went up soon afterwards."

"Thank you, Miss Welton. What about the other night? On which Lydia Mallister died?"

"So far as I can remember, nothing special. James was in hospital and I had been to see him in the afternoon. I went to bed quite early, I think, with a book. I did not hear of her death till the following evening, when I got back from work."

"What was your reaction?"

"It would be silly to pretend that for James and me it was not a relief. We knew she could not live more than a few days but . . . well, we're very much in love, Mr Deene. James had been devoted to her and did everything he could for her, but she really had a wicked tongue. You should talk to James. He will explain how we felt."

Carolus did talk to James Mallister, later that evening. He found him as frank, apparently, as Esmée Welton, but rather a colourless character.

"I don't think I've much to tell you," he said, "though, as I've told you, like everyone else, I'd like to help you get rid of all this doubt and suspicion. You know Esmée and I want to get married. You know I was in hospital when my wife died. You know about everyone's movements by now, I should think."

"No," said Carolus. "I don't know where you were when Sonia Reid died."

Mallister smiled. "Nor do I, quite, because I don't know what time it happened. Esmée went up to bed as soon as we came in. That must have been at ten or half past. I stayed up for half an hour or so, reading. Then I took myself off."

"Did you see anyone during that time?"

"Steve came in, I think. He usually did before eleven, after the pubs shut. Looked as though he'd had a drink, but not tight. That was quite normal. I don't think I saw anyone else."

"Did Lawson go up to bed?"

"I presume so. He went upstairs. Wait! Did the bishop cross the hall? He may have done. I can't be sure of that."

"And you went up about eleven?"

"I didn't look at my watch, but I should think so. I was awakened by the bell chiming by the front door, but decided to take no notice. It had happened before— holiday-makers desperate for rooms. Later the bishop came to my room and told me what had happened."

"You got up then?"

"Yes. The whole house seemed to be astir. When I reached the lounge, the police had just arrived."

"It must have been very disturbing."

"Well, yes. Of course neither Esmée nor I knew the girl well, but a thing like that is always a shock. She was so *very* much alive. Now may I ask you something? Do you think there was anything . . . irregular about my wife's death?"

Carolus considered. "I do, yes," he said at last.

"You mean you think she was murdered?"

"I just don't know, Mallister. If I knew she was, it would make the rest of this investigation much easier. But that's a question that could only be decided by a post-mortem."

"I wish they would have one then, and get it over."

"For all I know, they may consider both cases closed."

"We want to get away from all this," said Mallister. "Esmée and I want to go somewhere else entirely, when we get married. I can get a transfer from the bank. But we can't go till it's cleared up."

" I'm doing my best," said Carolus, " and you've both been very helpful. Perhaps it will come sooner than you think."

15

SINCE his arrival at Cat's Cradle, Carolus had felt that his best hope lay in the Jerrisons. He remembered Helena Gort's description of the garrulous wife and the husband who, Mrs Jerrison herself said, ' won't talk about it ', and felt there was something of a challenge here. There were other things that suggested the Jerrisons might have valuable knowledge. They never went to bed until late. ' We're nearly always the last to go up,' Mrs Jerrison had said. And Jerrison had followed Steve Lawson down to where the body lay on the night of Sonia's death.

He decided to make his approach through Jerrison and called him aside after dinner. " Would it be possible for me to have a word with you and Mrs Jerrison presently? "

To his surprise, Jerrison showed no hesitation or unwillingness. " Certainly, sir," he said. " Would you like to come along to our little sitting-room? It's through the kitchen."

" Thanks. What time would suit you? "

" Soon as we've got the dinner things out of the way. Say in an hour's time? "

If this was the untalkative Jerrison, what would his wife be like, wondered Carolus. But there he had a surprise. Mrs Jerrison was polite, too polite, and put

Carolus in a large armchair, but he felt at once that she had created what she meant to be an impregnable reserve.

After some minutes of difficult general conversation Carolus explained that he was, with Mrs Derosse's consent, trying to establish the facts about the two deaths.

"Well, I've told all I know to the police," said Mrs Jerrison.

"Of course. I should do the same. Only the things I would like to know may not be quite the same. Small things like those you told Mrs Gort."

"That was different," said Mrs Jerrison. "That was before Sonia Reid's death, and we didn't really know anything was wrong."

"Do we *know* now?"

"Well, you should ask yourself, sir. What with Miss Reid lying battered on the rocks and Mrs Derosse nearly out of her mind, and the police asking questions till you feel your head's going round, and Mr Lawson not paid his bill for I don't know how long, and Miss Grey near a breakdown—if that's not wrong I don't know what is."

"I meant, we don't know that Mrs Mallister did not die naturally and that Miss Reid's was not an accident."

"Accident!" said Mrs Jerrison. "But I've said enough. I don't want to make things worse than they are. We don't want any more 'accidents' happening."

"We certainly don't," said Carolus. "But I think they are more likely to be prevented by your telling me anything you know than by keeping it to yourself."

"It's not much," said Mrs Jerrison, clearly wavering. "And I've told the police."

"It might be vital."

"I don't know what to say. I'd made up my mind to keep my mouth shut. I don't want to cause trouble."

"Was it something about Mrs Mallister?"

"Oh no! That's all over long ago. I had to say at the inquest how I went into her room that night, as I always did, and saw her comfortable for the night. The only thing I didn't say didn't seem worth saying, really. She did mention then that she'd left us something in her will. I never dreamed it would be as much as it was and I never told anyone, because you don't know what they'd have made out of it if I'd said."

"I understand," said Carolus.

"She didn't say it nicely, either. She spoke as though she hated having to leave it us. 'It'll come to you and you won't have long to wait,' she snapped. I tried to make things pleasanter, but she wouldn't listen. So I made her comfortable and left her."

"You saw no one going to her room?"

"No. I didn't. I came straight down here. But that seems a long time ago, with all that's happened since." Suddenly Mrs Jerrison asked an unexpected question: "Is it known what time Sonia is supposed to have died?"

"As near as I can calculate from what the people in the boat told me, round about midnight."

Mrs Jerrison nodded thoughtfully.

"You might as well tell him, Belle," put in Mr Jerrison.

"It's nothing much. But it seems to haunt me somehow," said Mrs Jerrison. There was a long silence. Carolus was sure he had won. "We were in bed by twelve," said Mrs Jerrison. "Our bedroom's just above here, almost over the front door. When we've got our window open on a quiet night we can hear anyone moving about out there on the drive. Well, soon after we'd gone to bed I heard someone open the front door and step out. Whoever it was moved quietly and quickly at the same time. I thought it was a woman's steps. They moved away, but they were soon on the grass. I thought it must be someone who'd forgotten something from the terrace, and waited to hear them come back. But they didn't come—then, anyway. Of course, whoever it was could have gone right up the drive, keeping on the grass border. Or they could have gone round to the terrace as I thought. I just don't know."

"And did the footsteps return?" asked Carolus.

"Not for a long time they didn't. Must have been the best part of half an hour. Then I heard them come back. This time they seemed in more of a hurry. Whoever it was had a latchkey.

"Where I blame myself," went on Mrs Jerrison, "is for not having a look. Only, so far as I knew then, there was nothing wrong. I don't like to be thought nosy, looking out to see who's coming in or going out. But if I'd have just taken a look then, it might have saved all this trouble."

"You think the two lots of footsteps were of the same person?"

"That's a funny thing you should say that, but I've often wondered. You see, you don't notice things at the time. How was I to know that not long after I'd heard them these people from the boat were to come ringing the bell? But I have asked myself whether they were the same. The second time it sounded more like a man. But I can't be sure about either time."

Carolus looked at Mrs Jerrison and wondered whether she was going to break down. The big, good-natured face was distorted by her efforts to keep back her tears.

"Only there it is, Mr Deene," she said at last, "I can't forget those footsteps. It's like as though I could still hear them when we go up to bed at night. I'd like to leave this house and done with it, only it suits my husband, who's got weak lungs, and I shouldn't like to leave Mrs Derosse, not in the middle of all this. She's been very good to us, poor thing, and there is Mrs Mallister's money

148

to think of. But if it wasn't for that, we should go and double-quick, I can tell you."

"I fully understand," said Carolus.

"The wife worries over things," explained Jerrison. "I try to stop her, but it's no good."

"You'd worry if you'd heard what I did," said Mrs Jerrison. "And not know if it was a murderer or not."

"Well, even if it was?" argued Jerrison. "If there's a murderer in this house, you've seen whoever it is lots of times. And very likely chatted with him or her and made the bed and I don't know what. So why worry about those footsteps?"

"Oh be quiet, Redmond! You don't understand. It's nothing to laugh about either, as Mr Deene knows. You tell him what you told the police and stop giving me the horrors."

"Yes, there was something rather interesting," said Jerrison. "At least that plain-clothes copper seemed to find it interesting. He took a lot of notes about it. You see, Mr Deene, I was never much interested in this business. Not at first, that is, when it was only a matter of Mrs Mallister. I used to tell the wife not to keep on about it because it was all a lot of nonsense. But Sonia Reid was another matter. There was something very nasty about that. And what I'm going to tell you proves it.

"The first I knew that night was when I opened the door to that holiday-camp couple. I thought they'd pull the bell off the way they was carrying on. They began at me as soon as I opened. Excited they were—well, naturally. They'd come up the wider path from the beach, not our little cliff path that goes down. I called Mrs Derosse and she told me to phone the police, which I did. The guests started coming downstairs, some of them, and I went to tell the wife what had happened and tell her to get up and make a cup of tea. I thought they'd all need it. By the time I got back, they told me Steve Lawson had gone off and they thought he'd taken the cliff path to where the body was. So I took a torch and set off down."

"Yes?" said Carolus, for Jerrison had paused.

"You wouldn't happen to like a glass of beer, would you?" he asked Carolus. "It's all we've got here of our own. Of course I could go and get you . . ."

"No, no. Please. I'd love a glass of beer. Do go on."

"I never saw anything of Lawson till I reached the bottom of the cliff and saw him ahead of me. He didn't turn his head, but went on towards where the body would be if it had fallen from one of the rooms on that side. When we were getting near, he made a little dash forward and seemed to be going mad, jumping about like I don't know what. But before he did that I'd seen distinctly a set of footmarks going up to the body and back. Saw them distinctly with my torch. The sea hadn't been off the sand there half an hour, I shouldn't think. The surface was quite smooth, except for these footprints."

Carolus lit a cheroot, waited a few moments, then looked straight at Jerrison. "Now let's get this straight," he said. "You saw the footprints as you approached. Where were you when you saw them?"

"There wasn't much sand there," said Jerrison, "just a little piece perhaps five yards across with rocks all round it. I'll take you down tomorrow and show you the place. Our footpath, that's the private one from this house, goes down the slope—well, it's a bit more than a slope, a cliff slope, you might say—then crosses the rocks, which are smooth there and comes to this bit of sand. The cliff behind the sand is almost sheer, though. It looked as though the girl had fallen straight as a plummet on to the rocks between the foot of the cliff and the sand, then rolled or bounced on to the sand."

"Be quiet, will you, Redmond! Talking about people bouncing when they're dead like that."

"What's wrong? Mr Deene understands what I mean. Now, I saw the footprints with my torch while I was still crossing the rocks towards the patch of sand. There weren't many, because it wasn't large."

"And you had the impression that Lawson was trying to obliterate them?"

"That's what it looked like, the way he was jumping about. Of course he was half out of his mind and kept shouting 'Sonia!' and that. But there certainly wasn't much left of those footprints when he'd finished with them."

"Were they of a man or a woman?"

"It's hard to say, Mr Deene. I only saw them for a moment with my torch. I have the impression that they weren't large. Either a small man's, or a big woman's without high heels. But I might be wrong about that. And anyway it doesn't help much, because most of the men in this house have got smallish feet. Even the bishop. I remarked on it to the wife once when all their shoes were here for cleaning."

"Do you think they could have been Lawson's own?" asked Carolus.

"I had thought of that. You mean, if he'd started long enough before me, he'd have had time to get to the corpse and return to where I found him, pretending he was on his way to it? It's hard to say. It depends how long after him I left, and how quick he could go down that path without a torch. He'd used it often enough. But I've got another idea, Mr Deene."

"Yes?"

"Those footprints could have been made by whoever it was my wife heard. Her footsteps and my footprints could be of the same person."

"I wish you'd stop talking like that," said Mrs Jerrison. "You say Lawson was hysterical?"

"Worse than that. He was raving. Even when we started coming back and were half-way up the cliff he suddenly shouted 'I'm not going to leave her there! I won't!' And he ran back to where she was lying. I had to go back after him. When I reached him, he was crying like a child and I managed to get him home. Of course, whatever had happened, she was his girl, wasn't she? You can understand it."

"When he went back, what did he do?"

"Do? Nothing that I know of. I was busy finding my way across there again without breaking my neck. When I got there, he was just standing over her, crying."

"You've told all this to the police?"

"Not quite like I've told it to you, Mr Deene. I don't like the police, you see. Never have."

"Mr Deene'll think you've been in trouble with them," warned his wife.

"No. I've never been in trouble with them. I'm like a lot of other people, I don't like them. But I told them the gist of what I told you."

"Would you say Lawson had drunk a lot that night?"

"Hard to tell. He has been drinking lately. He's in money trouble, I think, apart from all this. When he came in at night, he was usually what you might call well away, but not drunk, really."

"He went on his own at night, usually? To the pub, I mean."

"Yes? Sonia Reid didn't like pub-crawling. I heard them have an argument about it once. But some evenings she'd get him to take her to the pictures or something. They were very thick, you know."

"Yes. I gather they were going to get married."

"I never heard that. The other two, yes; they talked

about it. Mallister and Esmée Welton, I mean. But we never knew Steve Lawson and Sonia were engaged though . . ."

"Now, Redmond!" said Mrs Jerrison.

"Well, it was obvious, wasn't it? I mean, they were living together."

"One other thing I'd like to ask you both. It's rather important, but I don't like asking because it may possibly seem to you to involve either Mrs Derosse or her niece. It is this. Did you see anything of Sonia between dinner-time and . . . the time her body was found that evening?"

The Jerrisons looked at one another.

"It doesn't involve Mrs Derosse or her niece," said Jerrison. "But I did see Sonia that night in rather a strange way. I was making my last rounds—about half-past eleven—when I noticed one of the guests' doors being opened very, very slowly. I dodged back round the corner of the passage and waited. Then I saw Sonia Reid peep out and, not seeing anyone, come right out and shut the door. I'm sure she never saw me at all."

"Whose room was it?" asked Carolus, expecting Jerrison to say Mrs Gort's.

"It was the door of the Natterleys' sitting-room," said Jerrison.

"Have you told anyone that?"

"No, sir," said Jerrison quickly.

"Have *you*, Mrs Jerrison?"

"No. I didn't take much notice of it at the time and, anyway, I told you I won't talk about the whole thing."

"Not even to the police?"

"No," said Jerrison.

"Then for God's sake don't repeat it to anyone! I mean that, Jerrison."

"You seem to take it very seriously, Mr Deene."

" I do. It is a matter of life and death. When the police have to be told, I'll tell them. Meanwhile, if you don't want another murder, say absolutely nothing about it."

They both looked somewhat awed.

" I shan't say anything," said Mrs Jerrison.

" You can count on me," added her husband.

Carolus had another glass of beer with them and went up to see Helena Gort. He wanted to know just how long after Steve Lawson ran out of the room that night Jerrison followed him. As usual Helena was accurate.

" Two to three minutes," she said, and Carolus had to be content with that.

16

It was past ten but Carolus decided that, in view of what he had just learned, he should not wait till the morning to see the Natterleys. He knocked on the door of their sitting-room and, after a moment, the Major opened it a few inches. " We were about to go to bed," he said, his face showing anxiety and intense curiosity. " Is it urgent? "

" It is, rather. You were good enough to tell me that, when I had reached a point at which your information would help, I should come to you. I reached that point suddenly, just now."

" Come in," said Major Natterley.

They both regarded Carolus inquisitively and he thought that their expressed willingness to confide really meant their anxiety to find out anything he could tell them. He was determined, therefore, to take the offensive at once. "You told me you had a certain amount of information which would be of the greatest importance to me. Could you tell me what it was?"

"We were speaking in general terms," said the Major. "As I explained to you, we have done our best not to become involved in the events which have disturbed this household. We do not care to associate ourselves . . ."

"But what was the important information, Major Natterley? It has become an urgent matter."

"Oh, little things we have noticed," said the Major airily.

"Such as?"

"We cannot call to mind at a moment's notice the very matters we intended to confide in you. After all, it is somewhat late and we are in the habit of retiring early. Perhaps tomorrow . . ."

"Tomorrow may be too late."

"Too late for what?" put in Dora Natterley with a sweetness Carolus disliked.

"Too late to prevent another incident, probably involving both of you."

"Involving us? You can't be serious. How can we possibly be involved in matters which we have been so careful to avoid?"

"I think you know the answer to that one, Major Natterley."

"You mean the matter of the Dormatoze tablets which Mrs Mallister was taking? That is simply told. Through a series of circumstances which, you may be sure, were quite fortuitous, since we never wish to pry into other people's affairs, we became aware that Sonia Reid had a supply of the tablets used by the late Mrs Mallister. We thought the circumstance most curious since they are rarely prescribed by doctors. Most unwisely, as we now think, we departed from our principles sufficiently to ask her about this, and she at first denied having any, then became rather rude."

"I do not mean the matter of the Dormatoze tablets," said Carolus. "I was fully aware of that."

"From Mrs Gort, no doubt?" He turned to his wife. "You see, my dear, how unwise it is to confide in anyone in this house? We shall not do so again."

"I think you will, Major Natterley. I think you will give me here and now certain information which you have so far concealed."

The Major rose to his feet. "Are you threatening us, sir?" he asked.

"Yes," said Carolus. Then, more calmly: "At least you are certainly being threatened, if not by me. You—or one of you—are in a situation of real danger."

"This is preposterous! How can *we* be in any danger?"

"You yourself have said that you believe a murderer often finds himself under the necessity of striking again."

"We may have said that, yes, and it seems more than likely that we were right, as events have shown. But it doesn't concern us."

"It didn't, last time."

The Major took a lofty attitude, not an easy matter for a small man. "So you are saying in effect that, unless we give you some so-called information which we are supposed to possess, our lives may be in danger?"

"Exactly."

"I've never heard such nonsense in my life," said Major Natterley, driven to the first person singular by his indignation. "I shall see the police in the morning."

"That would be the wisest thing you could possibly do," said Carolus. "But not in the morning. Tonight.

Now, Major Natterley. I suggest you phone them at once, for I may say that, if I fail to persuade you to confide either in them or me, I shall go to them at once."

"Are you suggesting that we have something to hide? Something to be ashamed of?"

"Only in so far as you have impeded the course of justice by failing to give all the relevant facts to those investigating."

It was possible that the Major might have held out, but at this point Dora Natterley began quietly to cry.

"You have upset my wife," said Major Natterley. "You come here late at night with a cock-and-bull story about our having dangerous information . . ."

Carolus knew that the man was weakening. Since he did not at once say 'I must ask you to leave', there was more to come.

"May we ask," the Major began again when he had patted his wife's shoulder and handed her a clean handkerchief, "what this supposed information concerns?"

Carolus had kept this, hoping that he would not have to fire it. But he gave it to them now, with both barrels as it were. "It concerns the visit made to you by Sonia Reid about an hour before her death."

He stopped, and there was silence in the room but for Dora's renewed sobs. At last the Major spoke—quite boldly in the circumstances.

"Oh that?" he said. "Why couldn't you say so? It does not seem much to make a fuss about. She did look in for a minute. What about it?"

"Have we got to go through all this, Major Natterley? Why on earth can't you be sensible about it? You know perfectly well the importance of that visit."

"Beyond the fact that we may have been the last people she spoke to, I can't see any importance."

"Why did she come here?"

"To inquire after my wife, who had complained of a headache that evening."

"But you were scarcely on speaking terms since the matter of the Dormatoze tablets?"

"That is an exaggeration. We did not dislike Sonia Reid. She was scarcely our sort, of course, but there was no hostility."

"What brought her here?"

"It would be interesting to know how you became aware that she . . . looked in for a moment."

"It is my business to know these things. I am also aware that she took every precaution against being seen. As you must have noticed."

"There was nothing extraordinary in the thing," said Major Natterley, regaining some of his composure. "We didn't think it worth mentioning to the police. She just looked in to ask how my wife was . . ."

"She was here for at least twenty minutes," said Carolus. This was his first piece of bluff, but it worked.

"She may have been. Time passes when one is chatting. We do not time our guests' visits."

"You don't intend to tell me why she came?"

"You know that. To inquire . . ."

"Major Natterley, I know why she came. And if you have any sense, you know I know why she came."

"You tell us, then," said the Major, still hoping that there was an element of bluff in Carolus which he could call.

"I will," said Carolus. "She wanted you to look after something for her."

There were renewed sobs from Dora and a look of real fury on the Major's face. "And why not, sir?" he said. "We are the kind of people to whom others can confide their valuables and their secrets. We are *not* the kind of people to reveal them to the first inquisitive snooper who comes here asking questions."

"So you accepted the sealed envelope?" said Carolus calmly.

"Certainly," said the Major defiantly. "Why should we refuse such a simple request?"

"You mean . . . you still have it?"

"It is in a safe deposit at our bank."

"You did not think it your duty after the girl's death to reveal these facts?"

"Mr Deene, we refuse to associate ourselves with police inquiries and things of that sort. If you feel that the envelope should now be opened, you may accompany us to the bank tomorrow and—since you are evidently aware of so much of this sordid matter—we will examine the contents together."

"I would give a great deal to do that," said Carolus, "but frankly I daren't. We should all be laying ourselves open to a serious charge. No, Major Natterley, there is only one course open to you. Go to the police station tomorrow morning as early as possible, ask for the C.I.D. man concerned in events at Cat's Cradle, and tell him about this. Make what excuse you like for not having done so before—that you did not realize the importance of it, or whatever you think best. He will go with you and take possession of the envelope."

"You really think that is necessary?"

"It is vital. For your own sake and your wife's."

"But what can be in this envelope of such moment?"

"I don't know, exactly, though I have an idea. I can tell you that it has already cost one and, in a sense, two lives."

Major Natterley looked sobered. "It is most distasteful for us . . ." he began.

"Murder *is* distasteful," said Carolus shortly.

159

Mrs Natterley was calmer now. In fact, the couple seemed to have found a kind of relief in having their secret drawn out of them.

"It is not that we are ungrateful for your warning," said Major Natterley. "We did not perhaps realize the full gravity of the matter."

"We *have* been a little uncomfortable about it," said his wife.

Carolus could not bear this complacency. "Uncomfortable?" he said. "I should like you to realize that, if it had not been for the discretion of two people in this house, you might well . . . Do you keep a revolver, Major Natterley?"

"We do," said the Major.

"Then keep it beside you tonight. And lock your doors. That may sound melodramatic, but it is a precaution I feel I must advise."

"We'll do as you say. We little thought when in a moment, which we see now to have been one of weakness, we agreed to keep this packet for the night . . ."

"So it was only for the night that Sonia asked you to keep it?"

"That's all. She said she would collect it first thing in the morning. Her room had already been searched, she said, and this was a private, family matter."

"That's interesting. Did she seem in a hurry?"

"She glanced at her watch a couple of times, certainly. Not very polite, we felt."

"She did not say whether or not she had asked anyone else to take charge of it?"

"No. She said nothing to that effect."

"Did she seem nervous?"

"Not really. She had, we had often noticed, a rather smirking way with her, as though she was continually getting the better of someone else."

"That, I think, was what she was trying to do, poor girl."

As though he was suggesting something eccentric, almost unheard-of, the Major said: "It is probably too late to offer you a drink, Deene?"

"Not in the least," replied Carolus. "A very happy thought. Just the time for my nightcap."

"What *is* your nightcap?" the Major asked apprehensively.

"Three fingers of Scotch and up to the brim with soda," said Carolus cheerfully and turned to the sideboard to assist the operation.

"Dora?" asked the Major, on safer ground now.

"We don't usually drink so late at night," Mrs Natterley said to Carolus, "but after the shock you have given us we should have something, I think. A brandy please, dear."

In the face of this the Major himself could scarcely refrain and with a whisky in his hand said rather lugubriously: "Cheerio!"

"Cheers!" retorted Carolus and tossed back his drink with hearty abandon. "Do you know," he said gaily, "I think I'll have another of those?" The Major scarcely entered into this festive spirit. "I shall sleep like a top now," said Carolus cheerfully as he was about to leave them. "By the way, would you phone me tomorrow when you've seen the police? I should just like to feel that's settled."

As he was on his way to bed he met Steve Lawson. He now understood those descriptions he had received from Mallister and Jerrison. Lawson was not drunk. Impossible to say that. But equally impossible not to know that he had been drinking.

"Good night," called Carolus, but he received no reply. After breakfast next morning he found Christine

Derosse. "I owe you an apology," he said. "I did a thing I hope I don't often do—jumped to a conclusion. I know now that Sonia Reid didn't ask a favour of you that night."

"But she did!" said Christine, smiling. "At least she wanted to. She met me in the hall and asked if she could talk to me about something. I said no. There was quite enough mystery about already without her adding to it with secret confidences. I never liked her, anyway."

"Do you still resent my trying to investigate this thing, Christine?"

"Not if you're getting anywhere." She looked at him squarely, "Are you?"

"I think so. At last. But I've had to let the key information go to the police."

"Bad luck! Why don't you tell me about it? After all, I can't very well be on your list of suspects, however much you keep an open mind; I wasn't here when Lydia Mallister died and hadn't been for months."

"You're not," said Carolus. Then added with a smile: "It goes against the grain to take anyone into one's confidence, though. Force of habit, I suppose."

Christine looked attractive that morning and, in spite of the anxiety she felt, she had not lost her gaiety. "You might try, Carolus."

Before he realized fully what he was doing, Carolus found himself deep in the story of his researches—what he had learned from his interview with the Grimburns; then his meeting with Mrs Tukes.

"I thought it was something like that," said Christine of Sonia's past history. "It's rather natural for a girl brought up in an orphanage and with that sort of foster-mother to put her own interests first all the time, isn't it? I meant to have a chat with Mrs Tukes when she came down for the funeral but missed her, afterwards. Go on."

Of Steve Lawson, Christine said: "Yes. That sounds right. He certainly had money once and he's pretty desperate for it now."

When he described his interview with Mrs Cremoine Rose, Christine said: "I could have saved you the trouble of that. We knew her."

"Not quite," said Carolus. "She told me there was madness in the family, as well as hereditary heart disease. She was thankful she was 'untouched by both'. But she maintained firmly that Lydia was very far from mentally normal when she died. What do you say about that?"

"May be true, in a way. She had quite an obsessional hatred of James."

Carolus went on to give Mr Cracknell's account of Bishop Grissell's past.

"We knew there was something of the sort, but a man who claimed to know the circumstances maintained that the bishop was only shielding his sister, who was really to blame."

At his account of Mr Topham of Conway Towers Preparatory School, Christine laughed outright. "That was absurd of you," she said. "Surely you could *see* that the Jerrisons are angels?"

They smiled over Esmée Welton having 'set her cap' at the bishop, but Christine said that, according to her aunt, there might be some truth in it. Finally, diffidently and under a particular promise of secrecy, Carolus told Christine of the Gees-Gees and their listening-post.

Christine was interested by his account of Mrs Jerrison's footsteps and Jerrison's footmarks, but made no comment. When he told her of Sonia's visit to the Natterleys she exclaimed at once: "So that's where she went with her confidence that night! It's very surprising."

"Is it?"

163

"She'd had a row with the Natterleys."

"I know. But where else could she go?"

"Mrs Gort."

"She had tried her."

"I see. Dora Natterley was the last chance. She must have been desperate."

"She was," said Carolus and told her about the two sealed envelopes.

Christine thought for a long time, then said: "But do you see *no* way of clearing this up, Carolus?"

"It may be that, when the police open that envelope, they will have the truth of it."

"And make an arrest?"

"Perhaps."

"When?"

"They won't move in a hurry. We don't know what facts they've already got. But it should be within forty-eight hours."

"By tomorrow evening?"

"I should think so."

"Then let me tell you, if they haven't done anything by then," Christine spoke with suppressed excitement, "I'm going to step in. I've got a plan, Carolus, which can't fail."

"I dare say you have, my dear girl, but I don't think you quite realize the dangers. If I am right in this case —and I've got little more than guesswork to support me —we have here the most dangerous of all kinds of murderer, one who is fighting for survival. One who will stop at absolutely nothing. One who can't stop now. I tell you solemnly, your life wouldn't be worth a light if you stuck your neck out in the way I guess you are proposing to do."

"I can look after myself," said Christine.

"That's what Sonia Reid thought."

"But I *can*, I know what I'm doing."

"Will you promise me one thing?"

"I doubt it. What?"

"That you'll tell me before you do anything?"

Christine considered. "Yes," she said. "I'll promise you that."

17

THE weather broke at last and it seemed that winter came almost in a night. When the household of Cat's Cradle went to bed that evening it was dark and gusty, and on the following morning there was steady rain with a leaden sky. There was something grim and final about this, as though, now that the long freakish spell of fine weather was over, there would be no more sunshine till the spring.

Carolus was called to the phone at eleven o'clock to hear Major Natterley's voice, elaborately casual, operating from Belstock.

"As it happened, Deene, it was a good thing you mentioned that little matter. The police were most grateful to us."

"They made no comment about not having heard earlier?"

"They did just remark that it could have been formally reported to the Coroner, but we explained that it had never occurred to us that it could be important."

"They gave you no idea of the contents of the envelope, of course?" Carolus asked, glad the telephone at Cat's Cradle was in a small sound-proof compartment.

"None whatever. Naturally we made no inquiry. We had no wish to associate ourselves . . ."

"This line's so bad," said Carolus and put the receiver down.

It was time he went to the police himself. It was his very firm conviction that, when he was in possession of facts which might aid them in their inquiries, it was his duty to reveal these. His theories were his own concern.

This had sometimes led to embarrassment when the C.I.D. man in charge of a case resented being told anything which Carolus might have discovered, but on the other occasions, especially when his friend John Moore was in charge, Carolus had found the police receptive; even, at times, in a cagey way, co-operative.

In this case, by persuading the Natterleys to hand over the envelope themselves, he had lost any chance of winning the interest of the police in his own efforts, and he had little concrete to offer them in the way of facts or discoveries. All the same, he decided to see Detective Inspector Brizzard, who was in charge. Nothing could be lost by it and perhaps he might gain, even by negative means, some inkling of what was in the envelope.

But when he rang up for an appointment he was warned at once of what to expect. "Have you some facts connected with these matters which you wish to communicate?" asked a cold and business-like voice.

"I don't know whether you would call them facts. There are certain things you ought to know."

"I can give you half an hour at four o'clock today," said Brizzard.

"I'll come down."

He parked the Bentley Continental outside the police station and was amused to note the prompt, probably prearranged, arrival of a constable, who told him quite civilly that it should be in a neighbouring car park. When at last, after waiting ten minutes, he was admitted into Brizzard's office, he found that they were not to be alone. Another plain-clothes man sat at a desk in the corner, apparently busy with papers.

Brizzard himself was a thin, sharp-faced man, intent on being business-like and maintaining a strictly official manner. "Sit down," he said. "You have some information for me?"

"Mind if I smoke?" asked Carolus, before lighting a cigarette. "No, I'm not sure I have now. I sent it you this morning."

"You . . . I don't understand, Mr Deene."

"I persuaded the Natterleys to bring you that envelope. They did so, I hope? They tell me they did."

Brizzard looked at him fixedly. Carolus was sure that the Inspector knew his reputation but did not intend to admit it.

"How do you come into this, Mr Deene?" he asked.

Two can play at that game, Carolus thought.

"I'm a guest in the house. Mrs Gort is a very old friend of mine."

"You mentioned an envelope."

"Yes. One of the two Sonia Reid had prepared on the night of her death."

"*Two?*" It was quite involuntary. A score to Carolus.

"Yes. Didn't you know that? Early in the evening she had two identical sealed envelopes in her bag. At least, they appeared identical, but she must have had some way of distinguishing them."

Carolus was delighted. He had learned one thing he wanted to know. For the second envelope, he reflected, might have remained in Sonia's handbag and so now be in the possession of the police. In that case Brizzard would never have let out his surprised and (Carolus was sure) quite spontaneous "Two?" Or it might, as he had long suspected and now believed, have been on her when she fell.

Brizzard did not know what he had done, evidently. "How do you know there were two?" he asked.

"My spies are everywhere," grinned Carolus infuriatingly.

"I am asking you a question, Mr Deene."

"I realize that. I have given you the information in my possession. How I came by it is my own affair. Sonia had two envelopes, one containing whatever it is you found this morning, the other, I imagine, blank. But that's only a guess. We know what happened to the important one. The thing is, what happened to the other?"

Brizzard fell back on his official position. "Is that all you have to tell me?" he asked.

Carolus ignored this and went on: "Because, you see, if Sonia was murdered for the contents of that envelope, and if the murderer only found the other and literally drew a blank, we're dealing with a still very dangerous killer, don't you think? I mean *I* was able to find out where those contents were—why shouldn't he or she?"

"I am interested in any facts you may have to give me, Mr Deene, not in speculations."

"Then here are some more for you. Lydia Mallister had two quarrels on the night she died, one minor one with Miss Grissell, and a real up-and-downer with Mrs Derosse. Her sister informs me that there is insanity in the family."

"For a casual guest in the house, Mr Deene, you seem to have made an unusually close study of its inmates."

"I have. It's the sort of thing that interests me intensely. I was born inquisitive."

"So I observe. I should like to know just what brought you to me this afternoon."

"It was a long chance," admitted Carolus. "I hadn't much hope that you'd play ball. But there *are* C.I.D. men who would have appreciated my resisting the temptation to open that envelope and my sending it to you intact, instead. There *are* C.I.D. men who would have told me what was in it."

"Oh, are there?" said Brizzard more truculently. "Then they would be guilty of a serious breach. I may tell you, Mr Deene, straight away, that I have no intention of discussing this case with you. So far as I am concerned, you are a guest in the house who has come to me with information. Its value is small, because you don't wish to tell me its source."

"I can tell you its source was reliable," said Carolus, "but I don't suppose you will take my word for that."

Brizzard pondered, then offered Carolus a cigarette. His manner became rather more conciliatory. "I think it is your duty to tell me, Mr Deene. I am responsible for the investigation of these events and you are not."

"Perhaps I feel as much responsibility as you, Inspector."

"I admit you may feel a certain moral responsibility, but it is I who would be held accountable for any further unpleasant events at the house. You must see that. If what you tell me is true, there is, as you have said, a situation which may well be dangerous. How do you *know* there were two envelopes?"

"I understand your position," Carolus said. "I even respect it. As you say, you would have to carry the can for another murder, both in your own conscience and publicly. This is the sort of thing that would mean questions in the Commons, and heaven knows what! I see all that. But to tell you how I know would be a breach of confidence. I simply can't do it. I can only say that I firmly believe it to be true and leave it at that. Besides, *is* it so important? Presuming there is a murderer, and that he or she is out for that envelope, whether a blank has turned up or not, the murderer must still be looking for the real one."

Brizzard assumed his poker face. " I'm sorry you won't tell me," he said. " Have a cup of tea? " He turned to the man at the other desk. " Tynan," he said, " see if you can get some tea. Meanwhile," he returned to Carolus, " is there anything else you have . . . chanced on while you have just been staying casually in that house? "

At last there was the faintest hint of a smile on his lips.

" I expect you know it all. That Sonia Reid had Dormatoze tablets? " Brizzard nodded. " The bishop's past. Yes? Lawson's debts and engagement to Sonia? "

" I didn't know they were actually engaged."

" I have only her foster-mother's word for it. Mrs Tukes, 17 Northumberland Terrace, Forest Hill." Brizzard took a note. " Mallister's colourless past and his wish to marry Esmée Welton and get away? You probably know more about Mallister than I do. I can find nothing of interest, though in a way he is the most deeply involved of all. I don't care for him much, though he seems popular in the household, doesn't he? "

Brizzard was not to be drawn.

" Sonia complaining that her room had been searched. Lydia's will. What the Grimburns saw—*ad nauseam*, I expect. Where everyone was at the relevant times, or where everyone says he was. The footsteps Mrs Jerrison heard and the footmarks Jerrison saw. It's all terribly insubstantial, isn't it? "

" It's a very curious case," said Brizzard.

They stirred their tea.

" I was hoping," tried Carolus brightly, " that the contents of that envelope would enable you to make an arrest."

He watched Brizzard closely, but there was no change of expression.

"I thought, in my artless way, that whatever was in it might be some proof that Lydia Mallister was murdered. Then it would all fit in. Sonia trying to blackmail . . ."

"You were wrong, Mr Deene. That envelope did not contain proof or even evidence that Mrs Mallister was murdered."

Carolus stared at the policeman, surprised that he should have said so much.

"So I shall have to begin all over again, shall I?" he grinned.

Brizzard's attitude seemed to indicate that the interview was over and Carolus went out into the wet evening to walk to his car.

Just as he was starting it, Esmée Welton came across. "My wretched car won't start," she said. "Will you give me a lift if you're going out to Cat's Cradle?"

She climbed in and went on talking. "I wanted to get home because James isn't well today," she said. "He stayed in his room. I don't think you realize what a strain this is for us all. Poor James has never been strong, and since that operation . . ."

"You're very fond of Mallister, aren't you, Esmée?"

She turned to Carolus, smiling. "That's an understatement," she said.

"Then give him a tip from me, will you? Tell him not to take any chances till this thing is cleared up. Not to be alone near the top of the cliff, or anything. To eat what we all do. You know, just ordinary precautions."

"Do you mean—James is in danger?"

"We're all in some danger, Esmée. All of us."

"But James in particular?"

"Mallister has not told me much," said Carolus. "If

he knows more than he has been willing to say to me or the police . . ."

"I don't think so. He is very frank. Oh, I wish it were all over. I long to get away from here."

They ran across from the car to the front door of Cat's Cradle, for now the rain was pelting down. The wind had dropped and the rain had that dreary persistent continuity which is noticeable when the night is still and the clouds low.

Esmée hurried upstairs but Carolus found himself stopped in the entrance hall by the formidable obstacle of an infuriated Phiz Grissell. She seemed unnaturally tall and menacing. "What do you *mean* by it?" she asked. "How *dare* you?"

Carolus guessed what had happened. "Good evening, Miss Grissell," he said. "Is there something wrong?"

"You know there is. Don't prevaricate. How dare you go to that miserable little buffoon Cracknell to ask questions about my brother? Is that the conduct of a gentleman?"

"No," said Carolus. "It is the conduct of someone determined to discover the truth, gentility or no."

"It is outrageous. You know perfectly well my brother is not concerned in all this jiggery-pokery here. Why go and question that insignificant little wretch Cracknell about him?"

"To be candid, Miss Grissell, I was not interested so much in your brother's story as in your own."

Miss Grissell snorted. Though few living men can know what the snort of a war-horse is like, it is safe to suggest a resemblance.

"Are you being impertinent?" she asked.

"If you like. The truth is, this kind of investigation and good manners have not much relationship."

"I think you're a cad," said Phiz.

"There will be many to agree with you."

"To go nosing into people's private lives. Especially by questioning that giggling little nonentity Cracknell. I have never liked or trusted him. I suppose he told you some cock-and-bull story about my brother?"

Carolus was suspicious. Did she really think that the reason for Bishop Grissell's resignation was a secret?

"He only told me things generally known," said Carolus, and left her.

18

MOST of the people at Cat's Cradle said afterwards they would remember what happened that night to the end of their lives. For one of them, at least, that meant a very short time in which to recall it.

The first significant event passed unnoticed by most members of the household, yet, as it afterwards appeared, it had an important place in the sequence. Against all precedent Christine Derosse called on Miss Godwin and Miss Grey just after they had gone up to their room to dress for dinner. Not even Mrs Derosse had often penetrated the stronghold of the two spinsters, yet her niece knocked loudly and long when they timidly at first made no answer, then called their names and her own and asked for admittance. She remained, as Mrs Jerrison 'couldn't help noticing', for at least half an hour.

The meeting of Mrs Derosse's guests in the lounge for a drink before dinner, which had once, as some remembered, been such a pleasant occasion, was almost sullen, though unusually complete. Perhaps the dark and rainy evening had discouraged other plans, or perhaps some presentiment of drama had brought them together, but all were there.

Mrs Gort sat talking to Mrs Derosse while the bishop and "Phiz my dear" remained aloof, looking rather fiercely about them and particularly at Carolus Deene. Miss Godwin and Miss Grey were also a little apart, but their isolation seemed, as usual, reserved rather than unfriendly. Carolus had a drink with James Mallister, who had decided to come down for dinner after resting in his room until now. Esmée joined them and talked with unnecessary gratitude of Carolus rescuing her that evening. Steve Lawson remained alone, knocking back three double gins, and the Natterleys arrived late and drank nothing, though—as at the drop of a hat they would have explained—they believed in putting in an appearance to show that they did not wish to be unsociable, however they might jointly feel about the gathering. Jerrison, inscrutable but competent and obliging, served drinks.

Conversation, however, did not 'hum' or 'buzz' or 'crackle' as it is reputed to do at cocktail parties; indeed it never became general at all, though the bishop could presently be heard recounting an incident that had befallen him in Pretoria—or was it Paulpietersburg, Patsankonda or Plattbeen?—to which the Gee-Gees listened politely. Carolus was absent-minded, though Mallister seemed to be making extraordinary efforts to maintain some kind of conversation with him. Everyone looked rather tense, but that had ceased to be unusual.

Dinner was chiefly notable for an argument between Christine and Carolus. She had at first resented his arrival and, though Carolus had taken her into his confidence, it seemed tonight that their early hostility was renewed.

It started with something Carolus said about the Merrydown Camp which Christine professed to find affected and highbrow. "It makes thousands of people happy; why should you gibe at it?" she asked.

"I don't. I was impressed. The organization is remarkable."

"Oh, don't be so precious!" said Christine, exasperated by this uncomforting praise.

They bickered on for some time until Christine let herself become more personal. "You're not even very good as a self-appointed investigator, Mr Deene. The police will get to the bottom of our troubles far sooner than you."

"Think so?" said Carolus.

"I *know* it. They will have the whole thing finished tomorrow, and you can go back to your school and teach history again and not try to interfere in the lives of other people." She was flushed and angry, but seemed to think that she had said too much. "I'm sorry if I was rude," she added. "I'm a bit het up tonight."

Miss Godwin stepped in with a diversion, evidently for the sake of peace. "Are you planning some alterations, Mrs Derosse? I saw two workmen in the house this afternoon."

Mrs Derosse seemed delighted with this. "Re-decoration," she said. "I meant to tell you all. They're starting with my room, to give you time to decide. If any of you would like your rooms done up, do let me know and choose your colour scheme. Your room I know wants doing, Bishop."

Bishop Grissell coughed. "I am not sure that we shall be staying here much longer," he announced. "It would scarcely be fair to ask you to decorate to our taste if we are leaving."

"Back to missionary work?" asked Christine mischievously.

" I've made no decision yet."

" What about your rooms, Mrs Natterley? "

The Major answered for her. " We, too, are uncertain about our movements," he said. " We rather feel that perhaps, now that currency is less restricted, we might try Madeira."

Mrs Derosse did not press her offer further. " Well, if any of you would like new decorations, I hope you will let me know," she said placidly.

When dinner was over, the Natterleys were the first to leave, but not before they had gone through their nightly performance of ' taking coffee ' with their fellow-guests and saying good night with marked formality. But tonight they were followed after a few minutes by Mallister, who reminded Mrs Derosse that he had not been well today and intended to have an early night.

Steve Lawson sprawled in an armchair in a corner of the room and Carolus wondered whether he was asleep, for his hand shaded his eyes as he lay. But quite suddenly he rose and with a surly ' good night ', addressed to the room in general, walked out.

There was a long silence after his going till Miss Godwin remarked: " I didn't hear Mr Lawson's car start up. He usually goes off in his car after dinner."

" I don't think you would hear it tonight, Miss Godwin," said Carolus, " with this rain coming down."

" Perhaps not. I notice he no longer has his large car," murmured Miss Grey absently, never ceasing her needlework.

" No. He sold the Jag," said Christine shortly.

To Carolus's relief this did not remind the bishop of someone who had sold a car in some remote corner of his former diocese; indeed the bishop had no reminiscence for them at all, and Phiz looked anything but chatty. After one feeble murmur to his sister that he did not remember rain like this since they were in Tamatave, he in turn took his departure, his sister with him. They looked pointedly away from Carolus as they said good night to Mrs Derosse and Christine. Even Helena Gort, presumably as a known friend of Carolus, incurred their displeasure.

Christine was the next to go. She kissed her aunt and and gave Carolus her hand. "No offence?" she said.

"No offence," said Carolus. "Take care of yourself, Christine. I mean that. You can laugh at anything you like about me, but not my warning to you."

Christine smiled. "When will you realize that women are not absolute fools?" she said. "Why should you think I can't take care of myself?"

"I believe you can; otherwise I shouldn't be sitting here. But . . ."

"Good night, Carolus," said Christine, and walked out of the room.

Miss Godwin looked up from her needlework and said archly: "I wonder why you are so concerned for Miss Derosse, Mr Deene. She seems a most self-reliant young person."

"I dare say she is," said Carolus.

"Mrs Derosse is quite happy about her, I'm sure," went on Miss Grey, "or she would not let her stay here."

Mrs Derosse seemed a little embarrassed by this, but managed to smile.

It was Helena Gort who spoke most frankly. "You're all in a state of nerves tonight," she said. "I've noticed it throughout the evening. I must say I feel somewhat uncomfortable myself. What is it in the air, Carolus? My imagination or the weather?"

"A little of each," said Carolus absently.

"Now, Carolus, you weren't listening. Will you *please* tell me what is wrong?"

Carolus stood up, and turned to Mrs Derosse. "It's too late to ask Jerrison," he said. "May I help myself to a Scotch?"

"Of course," said Mrs Derosse, and handed him the key of Jerrison's little bar under the stairs. "I think we should all like one. Mrs Gort?"

The three of them, the two elderly women and Carolus, drank. Of the three, Carolus seemed the most on edge. Usually a restful person, given to sitting quite still without fidgeting, he moved about the room in the most uncharacteristic way. Nearly half an hour passed but none of them seemed inclined to go up to bed. It was as though they awaited something.

Interruption when it came was violent. There was a thunder of steps on the stairs and the bishop burst into the room. His face was distorted with fear and horror. "Mrs Derosse—your niece!"

Mrs Derosse rose.

"I saw her go," shouted the bishop. "The door was open. The balcony!"

Carolus had already dashed from the room and, before the bishop had finished speaking, was at the top of the staircase. He made straight for the room in the tower, taking the second staircase in a few strides. There was no one in the room. The lights were full on, the windows to the balcony wide open, but no one was there. He went out to the balcony, peered over the edge for several moments. His arm went out in an uncharacteristically pathetic gesture, as though he could reclaim from the night what it had taken. He then re-entered the room, looked in the few places where a human being could hide, then closed the door and locked it. As he reached the landing, he saw that several guests had appeared there.

"I heard a scream!" said Miss Godwin.

"What has happened?" asked Esmée.

Carolus said something about an accident and went downstairs. Jerrison was in the hall, and Mrs Derosse spoke to him a little hysterically.

"Go down!" she said. "Christine—from the room in the tower. Like the other one. Please go down at once, Jerrison!"

"I will, Mrs Derosse," said Jerrison. "I'll wake Smithers and go down. We shall need to be two."

From behind Mrs Derosse the bishop suddenly spoke in his bass voice. "It's high tide," he said.

"As if that made any difference, from that height!" said Mrs Derosse hysterically. "You know the water scarcely covers the rocks. Not a hope!"

"I'm afraid not," said Bishop Grissell. "I meant only that Jerrison may not be able . . ."

"Jerrison will get there," said Mrs Derosse. "But there's no hope. No hope."

Then she turned to Carolus. "It has happened?" she said.

"Yes," said Carolus grimly. "It has happened."

He seemed almost to fall into a chair. It was perhaps unfortunate that it was at this moment that Phiz Grissell appeared, wearing a fur coat over her dressing-gown and looking monumentally wrathful. "You see what comes of it?" she said viciously to Carolus. "You see what comes of your amateur snooping? Another murder! I suppose you mean to see us all thrown over that balcony one after another, while you go nosing into things that don't concern you!"

"Phiz, my dear," said the bishop.

More of the guests now appeared. Mallister looked lost and unwell, the Natterleys frankly inquisitive.

"I thought I heard a scream," Mallister said.

"You did, Mr Mallister," said Miss Grissell wildly.

"Miss Derosse has been murdered as Sonia Reid was."

Carolus's voice cut icily through these hysterics. "Bishop Grissell, would you mind telling us exactly what happened?"

Miss Godwin and Miss Grey had joined the rest of them, well wrapped in dun-coloured garments. Mrs Jerrison interrupted by saying: "You oughtn't to have sent my husband out. Not with his lungs."

"There was no one else to go," said Mrs Derosse, fighting back tears.

"I should have thought Mr Deene . . ." said Miss Grissell, but Carolus interrupted her. "Now, Bishop?" he said curtly.

There was a curious lull. It seemed that everyone in the room waited on the bishop's words, though some of them could hardly have guessed the importance of his testimony. "I was under the necessity of leaving my room," began the bishop, "and going to the bathroom. Mine is almost the only guest's room in this house unprovided with . . . however, we will let that pass."

He seemed genuinely bewildered, as though he did not know where to start his story.

"At first the house seemed quite silent. I thought it was rather early for everyone to have retired. The rain, perhaps. But as I approached the foot of the small staircase running up to the room in the tower I thought I heard voices."

"Voices?" Carolus repeated to keep him on this point.

"Yes. Not loud. As though two people were speaking. Or someone talking to himself. The voices seemed to come from the room in the tower. I cannot be very sure or very clear about this. Perhaps I should just say that as I approached the foot of the staircase I heard, or thought I heard, someone speaking." The bishop showed distress.

"Go on," said Carolus.

"I looked upwards. Up the little staircase, I mean. The door at the top was open. I was sure the voices came from there. I don't know what went through my mind; perhaps something connected with the . . . other occasion. I started to mount the stairs and as I did so I saw Miss Derosse sitting on the balcony, exactly as . . ."

The bishop was overcome for a moment.

"But, the *rain*?" queried Carolus prosaically.

"The balcony roof covers it pretty well," put in Mrs Jerrison.

"I can only say what I saw," went on the bishop. "Miss Derosse sat there, just as we were told . . . Then suddenly she seemed to topple backwards and . . . disappeared."

"You heard her scream?"

The bishop stared at Carolus in a bewildered way. "I heard her scream, yes," he said.

"You seem doubtful about it."

"It's just that . . . she seemed to scream as she fell. It is all a little confused in my mind. I ran downstairs . . ."

"You didn't go up to the balcony?"

"No. I came to raise the alarm."

"I should have thought that would have been an instinctive reaction. To look over from where she fell."

"I think it crossed my mind. One scarcely knows what one is doing in such a moment. I could have seen nothing, of course. The night is inky-black. I came to raise the alarm."

"Have the police been called?" asked his sister.

There was some consternation, as it seemed that the police had *not* been called. Miss Grissell undertook this and strode out to the telephone.

Mrs Jerrison, in spite of her little outburst about her

husband, seemed chiefly concerned for Mrs Derosse, and sat beside her in an attempt to be comforting.

But Miss Grissell had not done with Carolus yet. "You realize what this means?" she asked furiously. "More questioning by the police. Another inquest. All because you like playing at detectives. I don't know how you can sit there asking questions. This is your fault, Mr Deene. Your fault!"

"I'm afraid it is," said Carolus wretchedly.

Esmée Welton was not interested in these recriminations. "James ought to be in bed," she said. "He's not well."

"It's all right, my dear," said Mallister.

"I think we should all wait for the police," said Carolus.

Though no one agreed verbally, they had all found seats and the ugly minutes began to pass.

"Only one of us is absent," remarked Miss Godwin unexpectedly. "Mr Lawson is not here."

Just then the front door slammed and Steve Lawson lurched in. "What's all this?" he asked at once.

Nobody answered him directly, but Miss Grissell said to Carolus: "You like asking questions. You consider yourself privileged to question everyone. Ask him where he has been!"

"The police will do that," said Carolus wearily. "I'll ask no more questions tonight."

From his appearance and behaviour it did not seem this time that Steve Lawson had 'had a few' or was 'a little high'. It was difficult to doubt that he was drunk. He sank into a chair and closed his eyes.

Carolus stood up. "May I open the window a little, Mrs Derosse?" he asked. "It's terribly stuffy in here."

He pulled the curtains back and opened one of the large Victorian windows, but, although there was scarcely any wind, the wet, dark night seemed to blow into the room.

"Shut it!" said Miss Grissell.

Carolus obeyed, but omitted to draw the heavy curtains, so that the rain was audible on the panes.

Suddenly Mallister, who was facing the windows, half rose in his chair and gave an ear-splitting screech. A shrill sound coming suddenly from a man is always rather horrible, and this was quite bloodcurdling. He turned white and it seemed he would faint.

"Brandy!" said Carolus and rushed out for the bottle. "Delayed shock," he explained as he poured some between Mallister's lips.

The colour came back slowly and Mallister began to speak in a low voice as though he was hypnotized. "I saw her," he said. "She's not dead. She was at the window."

Carolus whispered: "Who?"

"Not Lydia. *Not* the other one. She's not dead."

"Christine?" asked Carolus.

Mallister nodded.

"Ridiculous!" said Phiz Grissell. "My brother saw her go. Certain death."

"She was there," said Mallister obstinately.

Miss Grey caught her breath. "An apparition!" she said. "I've read of such things after a violent death."

"No. She was there," said Mallister. "I saw her distinctly."

Steve Lawson had fallen sideways in his chair. Mrs Jerrison was breathing heavily, as though her heart threatened to stop beating. Only Miss Grissell and Miss Godwin, both upright, seemed almost unmoved, their faces set in hard lines. Then, quite distinctly, there was a sharp tapping at the window and this time everyone turned to look.

Hazily visible behind the streaming window-panes, dishevelled and white, Christine Derosse stood watching them. There was an impression of blood and of seaweed, a gruesome spectacle.

There was a thud in the room. This time James Mallister had fainted. Esmée rushed to him. Bishop Grissell with wild distended eyes had perspiration on his forehead. Miss Grey covered her face. Steve Lawson had entirely collapsed. But no one spoke .for some moments.

19

NEARLY an hour later Detective Inspector Brizzard, Mrs Derosse, Mrs Gort, the Natterleys, the Jerrisons and Carolus were sitting with Christine, who looked perfectly composed and unharmed. Whether the rest of the guests were sleeping it would be hard to say, but with one exception, they had gone to their rooms after being assured that Christine's appearance had nothing supernatural about it. The one exception was already at Belstock Police Station.

"I'm afraid you have no alternative, Inspector, but to hear it from me," said Carolus.

The Inspector had started by questioning Mrs Derosse, Christine and Mrs Jerrison, but as all had referred him to Carolus he seemed resigned to listening.

"Make it short then, Mr Deene," he said.

"That's not easy," said Carolus. "There's a lot of dead wood to clear away in this case, and it is not even now what it appears to be.

"Let's start with tonight. What you all forgot, and I include the murderer, was something you perfectly well knew, and which I learned from Mrs Gort when I came into the case. Mrs Derosse was once a famous circus artiste and Christine is one of the few who have starred at both Harringay and Olympia. She has been called the Queen of the Trapeze. When Miss Godwin noticed strange workmen in the house this afternoon, she might, if she had been a little more experienced in circus ways, have realized that these were no ordinary painters and decorators. They were, in fact, two of the staff of the circus which will open this winter and in which, I am happy to say, Christine will star. Their normal work is setting up the framework of the net which, the circus proprietor insists, should be under Christine during her breath-taking act. Tonight, while we were at dinner, they were putting it, by a very ingenious piece of adaptation, under the balcony of the room in the tower, that is to say outwards from the balcony of Mrs Derosse's window. That explains Christine's survival. She learned how to fall into a net as a little girl and to her it is as easy as—falling off a log. Her appearance at the window of this room looking, we hoped, rather ghastly, was a little part of the scheme which did not quite come off. We thought that, on seeing her, the person who had flung her to what seemed certain death might conveniently break down and confess the crime. But there is quite enough evidence without that, as I am sure Detective Inspector Brizzard will recognize, when—if ever—I have finished."

"You've said it, not me," said Brizzard. "Please get on with it, Mr Deene."

"It is not easy to know where to start," admitted Carolus. "I was very fortunate when I first came here in being given details by someone as observant as Mrs Gort . . ."

He was again interrupted by the appearance of Jerrison, accompanied by two youngish men.

"Your husband did not have to go down to the foot of the cliffs tonight, Mrs Jerrison," explained Carolus. "He was in the secret. But Mrs Derosse had to appear to send him. Fred and Ray have been bringing in the net. When I looked over the edge of the balcony, Ray, as agreed, gave me a wave, and I responded. This was a signal that Christine was all right. My words to Mrs Derosse, 'It has happened', were prearranged to tell her that her niece was safe and sound. However, to get back to the story.

"I was so sure that Sonia Reid had been murdered that I used this as a working hypothesis. Moreover, it was fairly certain that she was murdered for information which she had, and for the contents of the sealed envelope. When I knew that she had made a replica of this, so that her bag contained two apparently identical envelopes, I could not doubt it.

"She knew that the murderer was anxious to get possession of whatever one of them held. But what she didn't know—and perhaps the murderer did not know it, either—was the length the murderer might go to obtain it. Her room had been searched for it unsuccessfully, but she never dreamed of any danger to herself.

"She was prepared to part with it for money, as a conversation between her and Steve Lawson, overheard by Mrs Gort, plainly showed. It was a 'thing of value to one person' she said, when she complained that her room had been searched.

"She was very sure of herself but, when she had made an appointment in her own room with the person she was blackmailing, she decided not to be in possession of the actual document at the time. She asked Mrs Gort and Christine to look after it, but both refused. She thought of the Natterleys because, although she was not on good terms with them, she could appeal to their self-importance."

"There's no need to be offensive, Deene," said the Major.

"Here she was successful. She left the envelope and went up to her room to await her victim. The appointment, suitably enough, was at midnight. Her victim came and an argument began.

"It was something said by Mrs Tukes, Sonia's foster-mother, which led me to see how the actual murder was carried out. She reported Sonia as boasting of her intelligence and saying: 'They'll have to come crawling on their knees before I give in. And then it won't be for nothing.' That's exactly what the murderer did. Pleaded literally on the knees for possession of the envelope. Sonia was sitting calmly on the stone-work of her balcony smoking a cigarette, entirely mistress of the situation, making her terms. That is why the Grimburns watching from their boat swore that she was alone at the time. Her victim and murderer pleaded, then perhaps, as Sonia mockingly refused to part with the document—putting it perhaps inside her dress—in a moment of exasperation, fury, fear or sheer madness, the murderer gripped her ankles and threw her to her death."

"How can you know that?" asked Brizzard quietly.

"I was pretty sure of it from the Grimburns' description of how she 'dived' over. That would be exactly consistent with her being propelled by the feet unexpectedly. But there is a better reason. The murderer, as you shall hear, repeated the performance.

"The interesting thing to me is that I am fairly sure that, in going to Sonia's room that night, the murderer had no idea of doing this. If ever there was a crime committed on an almost irresistible impulse, this was it.

187

"As soon as it was done, the envelope had to be recovered. Locking the door of Sonia's room and taking the key, the murderer hurried downstairs and, walking on tip-toe, as Mrs Jerrison heard . . ."

"There! I told you," said Mrs Jerrison in an awed voice.

"The murderer went down by the cliff path and retrieved the envelope from the dead body of Sonia, leaving the key of her room beside her. When Jerrison arrived, he saw the footmarks, but unfortunately had only a moment in which to observe them by the light of his torch, and could not be sure if they were of a man or a woman. They were 'small', but all the men of this household have small feet.

"It must have been a very terrible moment for the murderer when the contents of the envelope were seen to be blank. The real document now had double significance. It had its original meaning, which had been enough to cause one murder. But it now provided evidence, if not proof, of guilt in this second death. For it would show *who* needed it urgently enough to kill Sonia for it.

"*That* I saw very clearly, as soon as I came to make inquiries. The way to find out who had killed Sonia was to find out what was in that envelope. Unfortunately, when I found where the envelope was, in the Natterleys' keeping, I learned that their mistaken idea of honour had caused them to keep it intact, unmentioned to the police. I persuaded them to hand it over, and Inspector Brizzard, quite rightly, according to police rules, refused to tell me its contents. But I knew these by now."

Major Natterley interrupted. "It's fairly obvious, isn't it? The document showed that Lydia Mallister was murdered."

"No," said Carolus firmly. "Just the contrary. The danger of that document to the murderer of Sonia Reid was that it showed that Lydia Mallister was *not* murdered."

There was an awkward silence broken by Brizzard. "Now we're getting somewhere," he said.

"Lydia Mallister was, at least during her last illness, an extremely malicious woman. She hated her sister for having married a rich man; she hated and despised her husband and resented his health while she was dying; she quarrelled with Mrs Derosse, a most difficult person to quarrel with. Her sister maintains that she was not sane at this time and that there is insanity in the family. Whether or not that is true, she had an obsessional hatred of her husband. She cut him out of her will, leaving her money—without it, it would seem, much pleasure—chiefly to Miss Grissell and the Jerrisons.

"But she could not prevent James Mallister from obtaining the large sum of her life insurance, and this worried her. When she knew finally that she had only a few days to live, she made a plan to deprive him of it. She would commit suicide, which would render the life insurance agreement void, for the life insurance was not payable in the case of suicide.

"Christine told me that Lydia 'knew almost to the day' when she would die, and she had bitterly told two people that night that they 'would not have long to wait'.

"Whether she waited until she felt she was dying, or whether she so entirely believed in the certainty of her own death in a short time that she was prepared to forgo a few hours or days of life, we are not likely to know, for she had only one confidante—Sonia Reid.

"Their friendship sprang up in the last weeks of Lydia's life and began, like many less fateful friendships, with a mutual interest in music. But soon, as Mrs Jerrison put it, Sonia was 'up in her room at all hours'. I would guess that she had not told Sonia her plan when she asked her to obtain in London an extra supply of Dormatoze. Perhaps her plan was not then formed. But Sonia knew when the time came what Lydia intended to do and may have been with her when she wrote her suicide note. Lydia took her overdose of Dormatoze and, comfortably aware that she had found a way to deprive James Mallister of every benefit from her death, she no doubt peacefully died in the early hours of the morning. If she had felt the approach of the heart-attack which was supposed to kill her, she would surely have rung the bell which communicated with Mrs Derosse's room.

"But Sonia, as she had told her foster-mother, was no fool and had already seen a way to turn this to advantage. She was seen 'nipping back to her room' by Mrs Derosse at about half past twelve, but she returned to Lydia's room about three o'clock in the morning—as Miss Grey, a light sleeper, heard—and retrieved both the suicide note and the extra bottle of Dormatoze tablets. It was with this note that she set about blackmailing James Mallister. Unless he paid her half or most of the insurance money when he received it, she would show the insurance company that Lydia had not died naturally, but had committed suicide. Her resolve was strengthened by the fact that Steve Lawson, with whom she was living, was in desperate need of money and was urging her to come to an arrangement with Mallister.

"Mallister as a murderer interests me. He was apparently a rather dull little man who had at first loved his wife and even towards the end had suffered the onslaughts of her tongue with patience. He had been humiliated by Lydia and, when Sonia, too, treated him contemptuously, it was too much. He murdered her in a fit of temper, I think, rather than as part of a deep-laid scheme to get the money he felt rightfully his. I do not think that

Esmée's liverish sleepiness that night was more than a coincidence, though I may be wrong. When Mallister makes a full confession, as I feel sure he will, we shall know whether he made any plans at all. I think not. But he was cunning enough to hurry down the cliff path, obtain the envelope and return to his room in time to be awakened by the bishop and Christine after the Grimburns had given the alarm.

"Steve Lawson's part in the affair is not a noble one. He may have been genuinely distressed by Sonia's death, but he was quick to realize how and why it had come about, and to make up his mind to get what Sonia had failed to get. He saw Mallister's footmarks in the sand and, by pretending to be raving, tried to obliterate them before Jerrison could see them. But fortunately for the Natterleys he did not know to whom Sonia had given the real envelope."

"All very nice, Mr Deene," said Brizzard, "and I don't mind telling you now that the envelope contained Mrs Mallister's suicide note. But what made Mallister try to kill Miss Derosse tonight?"

"He has been in his room all day," said Carolus. "Between his room and Miss Godwin's and Miss Grey's is a wall so thick that two cupboards could be made in its thickness, one with doors in Miss Godwin's room and one with doors in his. When we found that the two old ladies could overhear conversations in the Mallisters' room from their cupboard, it was not unreasonable to suppose that he could do the same. Christine only had to go up there and knock and call loudly before entering to be fairly sure that Mallister would listen to what she had to tell the ladies during such an unusual visit. What she told them, of course, was that they need not worry any more, as everything would be cleared up by the police tomorrow. She said that Sonia had given *her* the sealed envelope and she was going to hand it to the police in the morning.

" She perhaps overdid it by pretending to quarrel with me at dinner and repeat that she knew the police would act tomorrow. Then she went up to her room and waited. Mallister was desperate by this time. It was no longer a matter of the money—he was trying to save his life. He walked into the trap. Christine insisted on his leaving the door open and, with the big table and table-cloth in the way, the bishop, looking up the staircase, saw only her fall. I tried to reach the room in time to find Mallister at least leaving it, but he was too quick for me, regaining his own room before I reached the landing."

Brizzard nodded. " Such larks are all very well for you," he said, " but I'd like to know what would happen if we were to do anything like that. Suppose Miss Derosse had been hurt? Or even missed the net? "

Christine smiled. " I take that chance every night of my professional life," she said, " but it's one in a million."

" Still, we couldn't have let you take it. You know that."

" You have other advantages," pointed out Carolus. " You've got the crucial document. I don't think you'll have much trouble," he added. " I think you'll get a full confession."

" So do I. But we'd have got that, anyway, without all this performance."

" It was a star performance," said Carolus, and it was his last comment on the affair.